Green and Purple Birds

with

Bright Orange Feet

Green and Purple Birds

with

Bright Orange Feet

George Callahan

First Edition 2020

Book Cover by Flor Figueroa
Illustration by Andrew Cherry

ISBN: 9798667196310

Published by George Callahan
GeorgeCallahanAuthor.com

For my dad, whose faith and patience are the greatest gifts
I've received.

One

SOMETHING OF A MUFFLED HOWL, a gnarled whisper of anxiety, pierced the dark room. The boy sat and listened to palms rustling and the sea foaming down the gold sand. He breathed in the soft, salted air and returned to sleep.

Outside, beyond their sturdy wood home and into the dark forest of palms, this gnarled whisper of anxiety ran in circles, in pursuit. It filled every pore of dirt and mocked any essence of wisdom.

Like the storm of a single cloud, it went away just as it had come. The boy would not remember it, the sea would not speak of it, and the day forest would look as it did each day to those of the gold sand.

It was a single word, spoken from a twisted tongue from deep in the forest. Then it was gone.

Two

WHERE THE SEA SETTLES FROM ITS WRATH and the winds of the gale slow to a soft breeze, there is an island. It is not a large island, nor is it particularly small. The people of this island live as the sea and wind around it. Settled from wrath and soft as sea moss, they go about.

Among the people of this island lived a small boy and his father and mother. The boy had a brother, but this brother lived in the forest with the Men practicing sneaking and hunting.

At night, the sea swelled to their sitting place; during the day, a soft breeze filled their sturdy wood home at the forest's edge.

When the sea swelled to their sitting place, small claws rose from the grassy sand and practiced their own sneaking and hunting. During the day, green and purple birds with bright orange feet hopped among the grasses and tapped the cool sea sand.

The moon spread an emerald glow across the sand and the sun warmed it gold.

The boy studied the sea and watched the claws from their sitting place as the emerald in the sky danced across the sand. When the green and purple birds with bright orange feet hopped among the grasses and tapped the cool sea sand, and when the sand of the island was warmed gold, he sat with his father and he watched his mother.

"Father," the boy would say, "when may I join my brother in the sneaking and hunting?"

The boy longed for adventure. He longed to dance with the claws by the emerald light and fly into the forest with the green and purple birds with bright orange feet. He explored the forest in his imagination, climbing tall palms and dancing over creeping vines. The boy imagined sleeping under canopy and splashing in cool streams, ever sneaking and hunting with the Men of the forest. He could not picture his brother's face but felt his presence in these daydreams. Together the two would dive into a deep, blue lake from the edge of a mountain and watch sunsets and share stories.

"Boy, you are too small to understand the sneaking and hunting. Someday I will show you," his father replied.

"Yes, Father. Thank you."

One night the boy was lulled to dream by his mother's song. On their sitting place, he fell into a deep sleep. In this dream, the boy stood at the forest's edge. His father and mother stood behind him, smiling. He stepped into the palms. The gold sand and green and purple birds with bright orange feet disappeared. He was alone and surrounded by forest.

The sound of his mother's song hummed through the branches of the canopy, but he did not know he was asleep.

The boy walked. He saw yellow lizards and brown frogs and tree creatures and forest deer as he meandered through the palms. The forest floor smells different than the gold sand, the boy thought. When these words echoed through the forest in a voice that wasn't his own, the boy was curious. "Is another here?" he asked aloud. There was no reply.

The boy meandered through the palms for a time; eventually, he found a small stream and bent to wash his face and drink. The stream was deep. He saw shells and fish teem near its floor. A felled palm, covered in moss and orange forest-cap, lay across the small stream. Vines hung from it and rested in the water, pulled by the current.

When he rose after washing his face and drinking, a man sat on the opposite bank. A white bird rested on his shoulder in stark contrast to the forest. "Hello!" said the boy.

"Why are you washing your face and drinking?" the man with hair like the boy's father's, long and brown, asked.

"I am tired. I have meandered through the palms for a time." The boy felt his words as he sat opposite these two.

"Why have you meandered through the palms?" The bird rested noble as the man spoke.

"I was in the forest. I live on the gold sand with the soft breeze and green and purple birds with bright orange feet."

"Why have you come to the forest, boy?" the man asked.

"I want to learn about the sneaking and hunting."

The bird leaned close to the man's ear and spoke.

"Your bird! He speaks like us? I have only seen the green and purple birds with bright orange feet that hop among the grasses, and they speak to each other, but not to me. Though I have listened, I could not understand."

"This bird speaks many languages and can influence many men." The man's voice was soft, and the boy thought of it like he did the sea breeze.

"May I speak to him?" the boy asked.

"Anyone may speak to him and he will speak back."

"I will think of something to say."

The man instructed the boy to rest on the bank for a time. The boy asked who the man was and how he found his bird and if the boy might find a talking bird too. The man told the boy they would discuss these later, on the journey.

"Which journey?" the boy asked. The man again instructed him to rest on the bank for a time. The boy closed his eyes and fell asleep on the bank.

The boy woke and found the sun brightening his bed place. That day after he dreamt, he sat with his father and watched his mother. When the sun was high, the boy spread himself on the gold sand and wondered about his dream friends. He wondered about their journey and imagined where they might take him. To the Men? Deep into the forest? Across the sea?

Many sunrises and sunsets passed, and the boy grew in strength and character. As the sun warmed the sand gold and the emerald sand of night hosted small claws, his arms became strong and lean. Still, he learned from his father and watched his mother. He never forgot his dream friends, the man and the white bird, and wondered if he would meet them again.

One day, when his dream was long past, the boy watched his mother prepare an orange fruit. She peeled the skin and rubbed it in her hands and smelled her hands. She breathed in, closed her eyes, and smiled. The boy thought this curious. She tasted the orange fruit and again closed her eyes and smiled.

The boy spent his afternoons running and swimming and climbing. He ran with the green and purple birds with bright orange feet and swam reefs away from the sand. He climbed the tallest palms to help his mother gather ripe nuts. One day, his father saw the boy run with the green and purple birds with bright orange feet and called to him, saying, "Soon, boy, you will fly with the birds!"

"May I?" the boy asked.

"No, boy, you were made to run."

"I would run well with the Men in the forest."

His father sighed and rested his hands on the boy's shoulders. The boy felt rough palms and worn fingertips and wondered what sort of adventures his father had seen. Had he lived with the Men? Had he climbed mountains and explored the island? The boy thought he could climb the tallest palms faster than his father, though he did not say it.

His father saw his daydreaming eyes. "Boy."

"I am here."

"I want to tell you a story."

The boy bid his father wait a moment so he could fetch a kiwi to enjoy. His father agreed, and the boy ran to his mother and asked if she had a kiwi. She did. The boy, a kiwi in hand, ran to his father, kicking gold sand high in the air with the excitement of a boy soon to hear a story.

"Here." The boy took a bite of the green flesh and handed the rest to his father.

"Many sunrises and sunsets past," his father said, "a man left his home on the island and walked onto the sea."

"He walked? Onto the sea?" The boy imagined walking on the sea, far from the sand. Fish and rays swirled around his rippling footfalls, and green and purple birds with bright orange feet rode a soft breeze in color. The boy laughed at such an adventure.

His father smiled. He sighed and said, "He walked for many days on the sea and endured many hard times for it."

"Why endure these?" the boy asked. Now his imagined adventure held danger. Currents pulled, and winds churned the sea, and he looked for the sun and yearned to see the color of the green and purple birds with bright orange feet.

"His home and his wife and his boy"—his father pointed to the boy—"were in danger of war-harm. He went to learn from the sea to prevent war-harm from reaching his family. The sea taught him patience and to listen."

The boy's imagination blurred. His face contorted as he tried to paint these words into his imagined adventure. He wondered if this story was a simple lesson, and his mind wandered.

"He returned home after walking many sunrises and sunsets on the sea and found his home destroyed. His wife and his boy"—again the father pointed to the boy—"were lost. He turned to the sea and smiled for them. Three emerald nights passed, and the man walked into the forest and vanished into the roots, moss, stone, and dirt."

"Our forest?" the boy asked, his curiosity renewed.

"Yes. This sea man's smile, boy, is why the Men practice sneaking and hunting in the forest."

"The Men hunt his smile?"

"The Men hunt what his smile means."

"What does his smile mean?"

"He found what he endured for," his father said.

"He learned something great. He smiled even with his wife and boy lost." The boy's mind skipped about his father's story.

"And for this something great, boy, this medicine for war-harm, the Men sneak and hunt in the forest."

Three

THE BOY QUESTIONED HIS FATHER about the story. Are he and his father and mother in danger on this sand? Will the Men teach them of war-harm? Will an enemy come here? How can they prevent war-harm?

"That is enough for you now, boy. You are small and cannot understand. One day I will show you," his father said.

"Yes, Father. Thank you."

The story of the sea man made the boy eager to grow, and he sat with his father longer and watched his mother longer and many sunrises and sunsets passed. "If I do as they and act as they, I will grow in understanding. Then I can join the Men in the forest."

Many more sunrises and sunsets past this conversation, when the emerald light in the sky danced across the sand and the small claws practiced their own sneaking and hunting, the boy sat and listened to his mother's song. Her gentle voice lulled him to a dream: he saw the Men sneaking through the forest in pursuit of a white shadow. The boy joined the Men in sneaking, and he felt his brother's presence. The boy danced over creeping vines and splashed in cool streams, and he climbed tall palms to see where the white shadow, shimmering in the warmth of the sun, hid. It captivated him and he ran after it, never able to make sense of its form and character. He ran like he did on the gold sand; he kicked wet moss and dirt and palm leaves high in the canopy with the excitement of a boy adventuring with purpose. The boy saw the Men and thought them quick and strong. The boy walked toward one and tried to speak, but his voice was buried in his throat.

He woke and said, "Mother?"

"I am here," she said, pausing in song.

"Why do the Men sneak and hunt a white shadow? One that shimmers? I saw it now in a dream!"

"Boy, you are too small to understand. Someday your father will show you." She resumed her song.

"Yes, Mother. Thank you."

The boy slept well that night as the claws did their own sneaking and hunting on the emerald sand.

The next day, as his mother prepared a fresh fruit and ripe nut meal for sunset, the boy allowed his wandering thoughts to rest with him on the gold sand under the warmth of the sun. He resolved to sit with his father longer and watch his mother longer. "Then will I learn of the sea man and the sneaking and hunting and the white shimmer."

His mother's hair became streaked with grey and his father grew in wisdom, and many sunrises and sunsets passed. The boy sat and watched and continued to run and swim and climb and grow in strength and character. More now than his mother, the boy gathered the farthest fresh fruits and the highest ripe nuts, and he swam in the sea often.

One day the boy swam in the sea from sunrise until late in the day. He came back and allowed the sun to warm him dry on the gold sand. His father approached and, as humor does not dissipate with wisdom, asked if the boy had yet received his gills. The boy laughed and asked if people can have gills. His father thought they could not. "Do you like more running under the green and purple birds with bright orange feet or swimming with the sea creatures?"

"I think I would like best to fly with the green and purple birds with bright orange feet," the boy said.

"Ah. Gills and wings, then." His father laughed.

The boy's hair was long, his arms strong, his legs lean, and his shoulders sturdy, and he was curious and adventurous, his father saw. The boy caught his gaze and looked away to the gold sand and their wood home.

"Will we and mother enjoy fresh kiwis with sunset?" the boy asked.

"Fresh kiwis and sweet chuara. Boy, you are old enough now. Your arms are strong and your legs lean, your feet callused, and still I see adventure and curiosity in your eyes, like that of many sunrises and sunsets ago."

The boy grinned and imagined himself in the forest with the Men. He would duck under low palms and dance around brown rocks, chasing the white shimmer. He would forage and learn from the Men who spent many sunrises and sunsets in the forest. His brother would show him blue lakes and grey mountains, and together they would run, ever after the elusive white shimmer. He pictured tall palms and forest deer and tried to remember the smell of the forest floor from his dream.

"Boy?"

"I am here." He was eager to hear what his wise father would say.

"You saw the white shimmer?" The boy's mother had told his father of the dream.

"Yes."

"I told you many sunrises and sunsets ago of the sneaking and hunting. The sea man walked into the forest and vanished into the roots and moss and stone and dirt. And now, the Men sneak and hunt to learn. The Men want to find the medicine for war-harm too."

"I remember," the boy said. "The sea man took the medicine for war-harm into the forest."

"The white shimmer you saw in your dream is that which the Men sneak and hunt. They believe this white shimmer is the sea man, alive in spirit in the forest."

The boy's eyes widened with interest. The white shimmer of his dream was no dream! He looked at the forest. A new wind of curiosity pulled through its palms and lapped at the familiar air above the gold sand.

His father continued: "When the white shimmer first appeared, the Men gave pursuit, believing it the sea man. They see his spirit in its charm. The white shimmer has danced in the forest for many sunrises and sunsets, always escaping the sneaking and hunting of the Men. Do you understand?"

"The white shimmer cannot be caught?" the boy asked.

"It need not be caught. It charms; it does not serve," his father warned.

The boy's eyes narrowed and his head tilted to one side. A green and purple bird with bright orange feet hopped nearby. "Why sneak and hunt, then? And what of war-harm?"

"The Men have been lured by something seen and exciting."

"Can we not tell them, the Men?"

"They believe the white shimmer is the sea man."

"Will they not listen? Can you not tell them?"

"I cannot. They are lost to what they see."

A soft breeze shifted the sea moss nearby and a second green and purple bird with bright orange feet joined the other. These hopped among the grasses of the gold sand.

Away from the two and near the forest, the boy's mother counted her fruits and ripe nuts. She put these in green grass baskets.

The sun was strong that day. The boy felt the warmth of the sun deep in his body and he shivered. He smiled and thanked the sun for warmth. He remembered the day he gathered ripe nuts in the tallest palms for his mother. He climbed, plucked the nuts, and dropped them below. Sweating and smiling, he spread out on top of the palm and felt the warmth of the sun. His mother would tell him to hurry from the palm, but he would not spend less than a few moments atop each. "Boy!" his mother would call. She would sing too. The memory of her singing and the warmth of the sun on the top of the tallest palms made the boy's smile turn to a laugh.

His father saw both the smile and the laugh and remembered the day the boy captured a small fish stuck in a sea pool. The boy was fascinated with his capture. How does it breathe? he asked. Can I keep it in a basket? How many colors of fish are there? This fish was red and yellow. A sunrise fish! the boy said. The fish belongs to the sea, the father taught. It gives the sea life and beauty, without which you and I and your mother would lose our joy in it. Let the fish to the sea, for the beauty and joy of this sea and our island.

"Father?" His father's mind drifted farther than the boy's.

"I am here."

"What, then, is the medicine for war-harm? All seems lost." He felt pity for his adventures and realized his father would never let him to the forest. He looked to the gold sand and to their sturdy wood home and back to the sea. Would he stay here until he was wise like his father?

"The medicine for war-harm *is* the sea man's smile. His smile moors us to our gold sand and to each other and it cannot be learned, only experienced. These three truths I pass to you."

His son looked pained to grasp his father's words.

His father attempted to relieve the pain of his young son: "The sea man's smile and its truths are the medicine for war-harm. The forest, where he vanished into the roots and moss and stone and dirt, is said to hold his life." His father motioned to the forest. It vibrated with energy when his father spoke of it. The boy longed to understand the forest. "Men, however, could not see the sea man with their eyes to learn from him; instead, they found the white shimmer and gave chase. It captivates those who cry for the tangible in the intangible. The sea man, boy, is of the island. He lives in the sand of this beach and the trees of that forest and the rocks and sea moss and fruits and ripe nuts and green and purple birds with bright orange feet and small claws. He is the life of the island, not a shimmer to be caught."

The boy looked at the loose sand clinging to his folded legs. He took a stone, after a creature, then touched the deep sand, packed under the weight of many tides, with both hands.

"When Men cannot see with their eyes to learn, they forget this simple truth. They follow other Men and pursue the white shimmer and are captivated by it. The sea man is the air and the sky and the water; he is you and me! His smile, this mystery, moors you and me and your mother and the Men and all others to the island and to each other, and it cannot be learned, only experienced."

The boy, with both of his hands touching the sun-warmed gold sand, looked at his father, his hands, and his mother, counting fruits and ripe nuts.

"What is the sea man's smile if it is the medicine for war-harm? Where is it?" the boy asked.

"It cannot be learned, boy. It must be experienced." His father smiled. "Always remember: the sea man is the sand and the palms and the rocks and sea moss and fresh fruits and ripe nuts and green and purple birds with bright orange feet and small claws and the air and the sky and the water. He is the forest deer and night birds and tree creatures. He is you and I."

Four

THE BOY WAS STRUCK SILENT the rest of the afternoon and into the evening.

Could the Men practice sneaking and hunting in vain? Was his wise father right to say the sea man is of the island, and all things on the island—and not in the white shimmer? The boy yearned for adventure and was captivated by the story of the mysterious sea man. He longed to dance with the claws by the emerald light and fly into the forest with the green and purple birds with bright orange feet.

The boy believed the spoken word of his wise father. He sang to the creatures of the sand and was fair to the tallest palms. He thanked the sea creatures for allowing him freedom in the water and became fond of the shells resting on the sea floor. He thought the sea man in all these.

Still, the Men of the forest, in their adventure and mystery, stayed. Why did they hunt the white shimmer? Could it be captured? Could his father know this when all the Men did not?

Many sunrises and sunsets passed, and the boy sat with his mother on their sitting place and enjoyed sun chuara. His mother tasted a lime. The boy watched her peel the skin and rub it in her hands and smell her hands. She breathed and closed her eyes and smiled. The boy remembered her doing this with the orange fruit. She tasted the lime and closed her eyes and smiled again. She opened her eyes and caught her son's curious stare.

"How do you find your sun chuara?" she asked.

"Sweet. Mother, do the Men sneak and hunt in vain?"

"What did your father say?"

"He said so. He said they are charmed by the white shimmer, but it does not serve. The medicine for war-harm is in the sea man's smile, but the sea man is of the island and all things on the island."

"Your father is wise."

"What then of our sunrises and sunsets?"

"Boy, you are still young and of the sand. The medicine for war-harm is tasted in patience and quiet," his mother said. "Do you have these?"

The boy thought hard. He sits with his father and watches his mother often; yes, he has patience. And he is quiet when his father speaks or when he lies on the sand and feels the warmth or when he swims the reefs. He is quiet. "I have these."

"Good. You will then find the medicine for war-harm."

Five

THE NEXT DAY the boy allowed the warmth of the sun to dry him after a sea swim.

He sat and looked across the water. The boy wondered what lay past. He looked behind him to the forest and wondered what lay within.

"Perhaps I'll go to the forest and see for myself," he said. He wondered of food and shelter and forest dangers. He did not know where the Men kept home or how he would find them.

He sunk his feet in the gold sand until they felt cool. Then his hands. The boy was rooted in the gold sand; he was of this place: their sturdy wood home, his mother's song, the reefs, the green and purple birds with bright orange feet and small claws, sea moss and palms, fresh fruits and ripe nuts. The boy felt strange to consider leaving.

He remembered his dream friends, the man with hair like his father's and the white bird which spoke man, and the boy wondered if he'd meet them again. They kept home in the forest, he supposed. His dream friends, the Men, and the white shimmer—every adventure to be had—kept home in the forest. He looked at the palms again, stretching away from the sea and away from their wood home.

"I'll stay," the boy decided. "The forest is a mystery. I will sit with my father longer and watch my mother longer. I will learn to be wise like my father and I will learn to keep strong with fresh fruits and ripe nuts. I will learn my mother's soft song."

He was adamant and satisfied. The weight of adventure and mystery lifted from his sturdy, tanned shoulders and he thought what to do next. There were other reefs to explore. He looked around and saw he was alone on the gold sand. His mother was preparing kiwis and chuara and his father was cracking ripe nuts out of the sun.

The boy swam out and away; he kept the gold sand on his right side and cut through the clear blue and green water with strong arms. The sea floor was as far below as two tall palms. The boy smiled in the salty water. A ray joined him, then a turtle, then a school of red and yellow and orange sunrise fish. The boy dove and felt the warmth of a sunrise surround him in the red and yellow and orange school. The fish danced and twirled and moved through the water with agility, and the boy marveled. The ray and turtle disappeared; he was alone with the sunrise fish. To his left and right, open clear water. Above and below, more clear water. The boy stayed under the sea for some time and enjoyed the silence of water and the sea creatures.

He surfaced, smiled, and floated under the sun. He rolled to study the sea floor and to see if he might find a rock or shell for his mother. Beneath the boy and outside his reach, a long and ominous creature frightened him. Not, at first, for its appearance or reputation, but its suddenness and closeness. The large sea creature dove toward the floor and when it flattened, the boy saw its shape.

His brother teased him about such sea creatures, and he had seen ones smaller around the reefs, but the sight of this large specter with tall and wide fins and black eyes and a long, sweeping tail froze the boy in fear. Does it know I am here? Is this one dangerous? The boy's questions drifted, unanswered, around his rigid body.

The fish continued its sweep of the floor in large circles. The boy yearned for a reef where smaller sea creatures swam. His heart beat fast and the boy was cold, even with the sun warming his back. He wondered if his father had ever seen such. He doubted it; his father did not frequent the sea or the reefs. No, the boy thought, his father would have stopped him from swimming if he knew of such creatures.

The large grey fish with tall and wide fins and black eyes and a long, sweeping tail meandered out of the boy's sight. Still afraid, he watched for a time to ensure the open water held no more secrets.

A small school of white-and-green fish joined him in a grassy swirl. Satisfied, the boy headed for the safety of the gold sand. He swam faster than he might have, less interested in the sea than the sand now. When he came to it, he stretched out and felt the warmth of the sun.

The boy looked about and saw he was far from their wood home. He did not know which gold sand he came to and looked for familiar palms or rocks. There were none. The boy lay in the warmth of the sun and felt his eyes grow heavy. His breathing slowed, and he let sleep come over him. He smiled for the warmth of the sun.

In his sleep, the boy was on the open water off the gold sand near their wood home. His father and mother watched from their sitting place as the boy swam and dove and floated. The sky darkened and the sea was made black. The many sea creatures vanished and the large grey fish with tall and wide fins and black eyes and a long, sweeping tail swam in circles around him. He froze in fear and his heart beat fast and his fingertips ached cold. Closer and closer the large grey fish circled. The boy looked to the gold sand, but it was gone, and he could only see water in all directions. Another large grey fish joined and another and another, and now four large grey fish circled the boy. He could not swim for his fear. Each fish dove and vanished in the dark water, and the boy's fear grew until he could not hold it in his chest. He cried out, waking from his dream.

The boy sat with heavy breathing. In front of him rested a white bird.

"Do not be afraid," the bird said.

The boy's large eyes and his muddled thoughts tried to make sense of the bird. He thought it might be his dream friend and tried to speak, but confusion and surprise held his tongue. The bird spoke man! the boy thought. It must be my dream friend. His mouth moved in silent surprise.

The bird blinked its eyes and flapped its wings to fly away. It flew high and over the sand and over the forest and disappeared where the forest and sky met.

The boy was struck silent, his mouth and eyes wide. My dream friends are real! he thought. The boy laughed and thought to get home to his father and mother and to tell them about his swim and his dream and the bird which spoke man. What was it the bird spoke?

" 'Do not be afraid,' " the boy remembered aloud.

He looked to the forest, where the bird made its way. The boy felt its mysterious pull. "Should I look past the first palms?" he asked himself. Would the bird ever visit him again?

The boy stood and walked to the forest's edge, where the first palms shifted in the soft breeze. A sand hopper touched his foot and the boy's heart pounded. He was tense and nervous.

"Do not be afraid," he said. The boy apologized to the sand hopper for his nervousness and looked to the forest. He turned and walked along it for a time. Is the forest dangerous? His father and mother spoke of it with caution. Plenty of others find it suitable to keep home. He wondered how many Men kept home in the forest. Only a few? Many? The boy pictured himself with them, sneaking and hunting after the white shimmer. He shook his head. If I go into the forest, the boy thought, I'll find my dream friends, not the Men and the charming white shimmer.

"I will only look and stay close to the sand," the boy decided.

He stepped past the first palms into the dense greens and browns of the forest where the Men practiced sneaking and hunting, toward the home of his dream friends and where, long ago and unbeknownst to the boy, his father and mother tasted the medicine for war-harm.

Six

THE FOREST FLOOR SMELLS different than the gold sand, the boy thought. When these words echoed through the forest in a voice that wasn't his own, the boy was curious. "Is another here?" he asked. There was no reply. He turned and looked about for the white bird.

Alive in color and activity, the forest reminded the boy of a sea reef. Fish were replaced by insects and brown frogs and yellow lizards and tree creatures, and the forest had its own coral and rock and plant life. The boy thought it wonderful, and he smiled. A stream trickled nearby, and he thought he might like the forest because it was like a sea reef, but he could breathe and did not have to return to the surface often.

"This small time in the forest is good," he said. "I will look longer."

The boy felt no hurry or fear and, the farther he walked, less time. A moment passed only when a brown frog croaked or a yellow lizard flashed, or when a tree creature cracked a fruit or a forest deer painted the green her own grey.

He wandered away from the gold sand, intrigued by the forest. Sunlight and rustling palms carried his smile onward through many moments until he sat to rest.

Darkness inched over the forest, starting in the nooks of the stream rock where he sat.

He thought to rest here for the sunset and continue his wandering at sunrise. The boy found a bed of wet moss and he laid it across the largest of the stream rocks. He washed his face and took long drinks of the cool stream—better than any stream he had drunk from—and closed his eyes to rest.

The cool stream water still wet his face when the boy heard voices. He sat and investigated the cavern the forest had become and, without fear, asked, "Is another here?" He wondered again if it might be the white bird.

"No," came a reply.

"No one," another said.

"Only you," said a third.

The boy sat straight and peered into the darkness. He could not find the source of the voices. Did they come from behind the vines? Back the way he came? He smiled and said, "I cannot be the only one here if I speak to you."

The voices gathered and considered what he said. The boy did not understand their considerations.

"I would be glad for company!" he said.

"No."

"Not ours."

"And we not yours."

"Then why are you here?" the boy asked.

"Why are you?" one replied.

"I followed a white bird which spoke man from the gold sand." The boy heard commotion behind the vines.

Long fingers attached to crooked wrists pulled at the vines with a slowness of caution and three tall figures crept forward. Each wore his white hair tied atop his head and their skin looked as if drenched in the salt and sun of the sea since before the boy's parents were born. Their faces shifted from his to the stream to the vines to the stream rocks and then to nothing. The boy thought each surprised at his own ability to stand and speak.

"There live here no white birds which speak man, only us and what lies beyond."

"What lies beyond?" the boy asked.

"Nothing we have seen," one replied.

"Can you show me the way?"

"Why are you?" another asked.

"Why am I what?"

"Why are you in the forest?"

The boy thought hard. He followed the white bird here from the sand. Why? He supposed it was for adventure and curiosity, and he supposed it was to find the medicine for war-harm. His mother said he would! And his wise father said it was in the sea man's smile, which was of the island. He said, "To find the medicine for war-harm."

One figure cackled and said he would show the boy.

I think he sounds like an old bird, the boy thought.

The middle of the three figures raised his hand and brought it hard across this one's head. He ran off, back through the vines, with the agility and clumsiness of a small grey forest deer. This one's wailing rang through the forest, clenching any sleeping creatures' dreams with dread and pain.

"He did not need that," the boy said.

"How do you know?" the one who struck asked. His voice quivered with shame and his eyes narrowed and widened and shifted about.

These three are strange, the boy thought.

"Follow us; we have another like you!" the two remaining said with one voice.

"I will," the boy said. He slid from his stream rock, put the wet moss where he found it, and followed the two after the wailing of the third. The two figures moved through the dark forest with such speed the boy had to ask them to slow. They did and he kept with the two, though he was labored. The two's faces shifted and twitched as restless and upset, though their words showed neither of these. The boy thought them curious and wondered where the wailing creature wandered.

"Where are we going?"

"After our other," one replied.

"Where has your other gone?"

"Wailing. I hit him."

The boy resolved to wait and see and so they carried on. He reminded them again he was much shorter than they, and one offered to carry him. He said it was a bad idea and the one who offered stared at him for too long; for the first time, the boy saw the eyes of one close. Hollow yellow eyes, brightened by the emerald light above the dark forest, hosted long black slits. He saw this one smiling a wide, open grin with dull teeth too far apart to serve any real purpose. He could not see a nose, and the length of the smile and the distance between the hollow yellow eyes grew longer as the face stared. It was the first time since the large grey fish that the boy's heart beat fast with fear. These three made him uncomfortable.

The one who stared pointed a long finger into the dark forest and they carried on.

The boy had enough when they reached the wailing one. This one apologized—though the boy did not know what for—and put a hat of palms on his head. The boy thanked him and wondered if he looked nice in the hat. He felt silly for wondering so; there was no other here to impress.

"Why aren't you wearing hats?" he asked the three.

None replied. Instead, they each sat, and one said "Cobnuts!" to what the boy saw as a stone hut behind them, draped in nightmarish, shadowy darkness. The only response was a night bird loo. Louder now and with a shriek of pain, "Cobnuts!"

"Shall I get them for you?" the boy asked. Their faces—the hollow yellow eyes with black slits and long, toothy grins—hid in this part of the dark forest. Still, their manner was frightful.

"We have another to get them," one replied.

"Hello, I am Dahlia," a voice said from behind the boy.

"Greet this boy," one figure said, pointing a long finger at the boy.

"I have," Dahlia replied. "Have a cobnut."

Dahlia tossed cobnuts to the three figures. Their long fingers groped the floor and they turned slender backs to the two, eating as starving animals ashamed to be so hungry.

The boy saw this stranger wore a vine around the neck. It was tight and looked uncomfortable.

"This boy seeks the Men too," one, turning toward the pair, said to Dahlia.

Dahlia looked at the three eating as starving animals with pity, curiosity, and concern and said, while tugging at the vine around the neck, "I would go see the Men if I could leave."

"Who for the cobnuts? Who for the lime stem?"

The boy saw the three had affection for this Dahlia, and he thought the forest a strange place.

"I have not been to leave to look for lime stem!" Dahlia said.

"Tomorrow," one replied.

The boy felt tired and thought not to ask about the lime stem or if he might taste cobnuts or if he could leave. The three fell asleep in a heap of slender limbs and thin frames, and he and Dahlia sat in silence. He was warned not to wake them. The boy and Dahlia fell asleep on beds of wet moss.

THE SUNRISE CAME and the boy saw Dahlia still sleeping and the sleeping heap gone. Forest creatures stirred around their resting place. He heard a stream through the palms and vines and stirring creatures. The stream of yesterday, he thought.

Dahlia slept. The boy noticed the vine around the neck was cut free and lay nearby. If he could have asked the forest floor of its memory, the three figures would be forgotten; it looked undisturbed and not trodden. The boy would have guessed they were not real if he had not seen the long fingers and white hair tied atop heads himself.

He remembered the yellow eyes and the grin, and the forest felt cold for a moment.

Dahlia woke and laughed at the cut vine lying nearby and the boy laughed too, though he did not know why. "Were they real?" he asked.

"They are," Dahlia said. "Unfortunate and curious, they are. Clumsy and sensitive and violent."

"Violent?"

"Quite! Therefore, we sat in silence while they slept."

The boy was glad not to have woken the three. "I think I would like to leave."

Dahlia looked at the vine and said, "Tonight I am leaving them. It would please me to have company."

"They bid you leave?"

"I have been with them for many sunrises and sunsets, subject to their needs and violence. I often go and find lime stem for them. Tonight, I will leave by this lime stem," Dahlia said.

"Where are they now?"

"I have never seen them with the sun; they return through the forest at night."

"May we leave now, then?"

"I tried and I could not find a safe place. They found me at night; they have affection for me." Dahlia blushed.

"What then of the lime stem?"

"These three hold lime stem for most a night. Its thorns make them happy."

The boy thought of his mother's old lime tree. He touched a thorn once. "Happy?"

"Have you tried it?"

"Only for a moment on my mother's old lime tree."

"It hurts."

"What will this do for your escape?" the boy asked.

"There is a red insect that lives under moss. I have seen a frog eat it and remain paralyzed for three sunrises. It sat and baked in the sun, though it did not look sad. The frog smiled."

The boy understood and helped Dahlia gather red insects into a palm bowl. Dahlia crushed them and stirred them, and he felt bad; his wise father said the sea man was of the island and all things on the island. These red insects living under moss were of the island and lived on it. He thought, though, Dahlia ought not to live captive to the three figures.

After creating a fine red insect paste, the two went to find lime stem. It was easy to find. They gathered the amount Dahlia knew and headed back to where the three would return through the forest at night. Dahlia moved the lime stem through the red insect paste and told the boy about the three, though little was known.

"They are poor creatures, once like us maybe, now fascinated with the lime stem and afraid of the warmth of the sun. I do not know how they came to be. They speak of little."

The boy was glad to have come with the three and met Dahlia; his friend knew much, and he was glad for the company. He was also glad Dahlia planned escape; the three became unsettling the more they were discussed and the more he remembered the eyes and grin. He looked over his shoulder often as the lime stem was prepared, waiting for the clumsy and sensitive and violent and slender creatures to return.

Dahlia noticed his cautious looking and said, "They will not return until it is dark. I hope they have not found another."

"Do they often find others?" the boy asked.

"No."

The boy and Dahlia sat in silence until they heard the wretched voices of paranoia and confusion moving through the darkening forest. One was crying and another laughed as they came. Still in the dark of the canopy, the boy could only see tall figures with white hair tied atop their heads. Slender arms and legs and long fingers hung from lean, dark bodies. No dull teeth or yellow eyes were visible in the dark.

"Have you lime for me to touch?" one asked. "The boy should touch."

"I, too."

The one crying stopped at the talk of the lime.

"I have enough for you. He will not touch," Dahlia said. "Sit."

The three sat like obedient children waiting for permission to play chase. The boy thought he saw them smiling those smiles, but for the darkness he was unsure. One itched his leg and continued to itch until it was unnecessary, and the boy asked if he was well. The one itching asked if the boy would help and Dahlia interrupted, saying the boy would not. One figure raised his hand and brought it hard across this one's head. The boy thought it must be the same two from the night before: the striker and the one struck. The one struck cried and moaned until Dahlia brought the lime stem. The boy was fascinated at their possession and character. He thought them curious and more frightening as the night went.

Dahlia laid a branch of lime stem in front of each. Each scooted forward using their arms until they were near on top. The boy watched as the three faces looked to Dahlia, waiting for permission to enjoy the thick green thorns. When a branch rustled and emerald light shone into this dark part of forest, the boy saw one figure staring at him, though its face stayed turned toward Dahlia.

The boy sat, stared at by hollow yellow eyes and their black slit pupils. Its smile spread as the boy looked back, and it itched its leg with deep anxiety, never looking from the boy.

He swallowed hard and looked away, eager to leave the dreadful creatures.

"Go sing and dance," Dahlia said.

Each grabbed his lot and they scooted back into the darkness.

The boy and Dahlia, as planned, sat and spoke without fear of being heard.

"They tell me often of the singing and dancing that takes place when they have the lime stem," Dahlia said. "I thought it was a mind trick, but now I think they are singing and dancing somewhere far away, holding the stem close. They cannot hear us or see us, though their ears and eyes are open."

The boy looked at the three with careful eyes. Dahlia asked if he wanted a closer look. He thought not and Dahlia agreed with his decision.

"When will we leave?" the boy asked.

"I am ready," Dahlia replied.

"Good. And if they wake?" The boy looked at the three and thought 'wake' not the right word. "If they come?"

"We will run, and we will be caught. And they have promised to take me with them to sing and dance in the lime stem if I am caught leaving."

Seven

THE BOY AND DAHLIA, without caution for sound, made way back toward the stream. The boy thought they might return to the gold sand and see his father and mother. He said Dahlia could stay for some sunrises and sunsets and find another way through the forest to the Men. He talked about sun chuara and kiwis and their wood home and his mother's soft song. Dahlia was delighted by the thought but would not leave the forest.

"For a short time?" the boy asked, eager to see his father and mother and leave this dark place. Could the sea man be of the island and all things on the island with frightful creatures like those in the forest? He did not know.

"I am here after the white shimmer, the sea man. I will find the Men."

"I will go with you," the boy said. "I have not seen much of this forest and with those three asleep in the lime stem, I am sure you will find the Men. I will meet them too."

"I am glad for your company."

The two reached the stream as a heavy darkness fell through the canopy. The boy thought to move on from the stream and get far away from the three figures.

"Rest and drink a bit now, friend," Dahlia said. "Do not sleep though."

The two lay on the ground near the stream. One fell asleep and then the other. The forest stirred over the two fugitives and the stream trickled.

The boy came awake. The forest felt cold. He heard an unusual noise from where the pair came.

"Dahlia," the boy said.

Dahlia stirred and fell back into sleep.

The boy repeated, "Dahlia."

Dahlia sat. "What is it, friend?"

"Listen."

Each peered into the darkness of the forest from where they came. Palms and leaves and stones and roots all painted a black texture. The trickling of the stream and rustling of palms settled. The sound became clear, though far away. It was the shriek of an animal.

"A forest deer?" the boy asked. "Giving life? Or stuck?"

"We should leave," Dahlia said. The forest air was thick and cold.

"The three?" the boy asked.

"It is the one who itched."

"You know?"

"I know."

Dahlia said to move along the stream and be quiet and quick; sunrise would bring hope. The boy was as frightened as his new friend sounded.

The shriek grew faint as the two followed the stream away from the sea and away from the three figures, but it never ceased.

"Could the red paste have not taken?" the boy asked.

"I do not know," Dahlia said. "It was a game to try."

The boy and Dahlia moved for some time and the shriek grew louder. Palms shook behind and away. Fright seized the boy; he asked if the two might hide among stream rock and wait for sunrise. Dahlia said they could not hide, only move. The boy trusted Dahlia and he moved.

The shriek sounded confused and violent and the boy thought of what he might say when the two were caught and captive. He wondered if he would wear a vine around the neck. His hands found his neck and felt the freedom of no vine. He thought of the hollow yellow eyes with black slits and the wide, open grin with dull teeth too far apart to serve any real purpose. He thought the shriek must come from an animal. Still, the two moved.

"We've come far," Dahlia said after some time.

"It comes closer," the boy said.

Dahlia's eyes pleaded with the dark canopy overhead and the black sky behind it. "Sunrise is far off."

"Do not be afraid," the boy said, though he knew not from where it came.

"I want to find the Men and practice sneaking and hunting and see the white shimmer. I do not want to sing and dance in the lime stem with those three."

The boy did not know what he wanted, but he knew what he did not want, and he and Dahlia felt the same about what they did not want. Closer and closer came the shrieking and rustling of palms. How could a creature hold such a noise this long? The boy thought his wise father might have been wrong about the sea man being of the island and *all* things on it. He wondered if his father had been into the forest. Had he seen these?

The two stopped in an opening of palms where the stream widened and flowed smooth. Dahlia's face looked dirty and scratched under the emerald light. The boy wondered if his father and mother looked at the same emerald light. He felt sad for their demise and again touched his neck. "Do not be afraid," the boy said again, though again he knew not from where it came. Dahlia heard him and looked at him, then past.

There the stream dropped over a small ledge. Resting on a felled palm near this ledge was a white bird. Dahlia's face did not hide surprise in seeing the bright feathers.

"Look," Dahlia said.

"My friend!" The boy walked toward the bird and it fluttered to the bottom of the ledge out of sight. When the boy looked over the ledge, the bird hopped through the flowing water into a mossy crevice. "Dahlia, come."

"Let's cross the stream and move along," Dahlia said.

Before the boy could explain the significance of the white bird, the shriek fell upon them. Crashing through the palms where Dahlia and the boy entered the opening was a tall figure with slender arms and legs and long fingers attached to crooked wrists. The boy saw it now, though it had not yet seen them. The shriek stopped and the figure approached the stream and bent over at the waist until its head was underwater. When it stood, it saw the boy and Dahlia, both rigid with fright.

"Cobnuts!" the figure shrieked. "Cobnuts and stories and lime stem!"

"Dahlia, come with me," the boy said.

"Dahlia!" the figure mimicked. "Come with me."

The boy saw hollow yellow eyes bulging from a wide face with black slits that looked at nothing. The figure's smile was bright red, as if kissed by coral from the sea. Its dull teeth were spaced so the wide mouth looked near empty. White hair, no longer tied atop the head, hung to its starved shoulders.

It ran toward the boy and Dahlia, stopped to itch its slender leg, and ran again. For its speed, the fiend might have been part forest deer, haunted by the lime stem.

The boy pulled Dahlia from the ledge with a thumping crash of loose, flat rocks. The two clambered through the flowing water. There, a crevice, and the white bird. The bird looked at the boy. The boy looked back with curiosity. The bird looked at Dahlia. Dahlia's eyes stayed on where the creature's gnarled hand would soon reach in. The bird hopped again through the flowing water, resting outside.

"We're safe here," the boy said.

"I think not," Dahlia said. "We might have ran on."

The boy saw his friend's hands shake and he held them. Together they waited and listened to the confused ramblings of the curious figure above. It was an angry whisper, a ghoulish shriek, a frightful language of misery.

It fell from the ledge and cried, a horrible and chilling weeping. The boy was fascinated by these figures and thought about what to call them. It looked pitiful out there crying. The crying, however, was short. Soon the figure was speaking to Dahlia, though it did not see where they hid. It muttered about nothing the boy understood and looked to smell the air, hunting for the hopeless and afraid.

The figure saw the white bird.

Eight

As if aware of its own confusion and frightfulness, the figure fell into silent agony. It looked to see itself in the eyes of the white bird and was ashamed. In silence, it thought only of itself, no longer the boy and Dahlia.

The white bird rested noble and the fiend writhed.

When the sunrise rid the forest of darkness and fear, the figure and its silent agony were gone.

"Curious creatures," the boy said, letting the water fall over him.

"I'm glad they are rid of me."

"And me!" the boy said.

"Yes, I suppose I am glad of that too. Though it may do one good to live with such wretched creatures for a time. Would you go back?"

"I will not."

The two laughed and neither spoke of the white bird. Dahlia did not ask, and the boy did not wonder. Dahlia might have thought it the creature's curious nature to have fallen into silent agony; the boy felt it may have been too. He knew the white bird, his dream friend, hid the pair, though he was not sure if it protected. The boy let these thoughts pass and enjoyed his new company, Dahlia and daytime.

That day, the boy and Dahlia walked the stream, always away from the sea, and shared stories. Dahlia spoke of adventure, of blue lakes and red sand and endless fields of purple blossoms hidden deep in the forest. The boy thought he would like to see these.

With these stories, he longed for adventure as if he were small again. He imagined flying high with the green and purple birds with bright orange feet and dancing with the small claws by the emerald light.

The two rested under a cobnut tree and the boy slept. When he woke, two kiwis lay in his lap. Dahlia was gone. The boy thought his new friend strange for leaving without telling him goodbye, but this forest was a strange place.

"Two kiwis mean goodbye," the boy said.

As he said this, Dahlia came through a spread of vines. Each hand was wrapped around roots and greens.

"Friend! I found a rubyroot patch. I am glad to see you are rested," Dahlia said.

"I have never had a rubyroot." The boy was relieved to see Dahlia. Two kiwis do not mean goodbye, he thought.

"Their purple-veined leaves are beautiful, would you say?"

"I would," the boy said.

"And here, try this. The root is sweet as kiwi." Dahlia rinsed the root in the cool stream near the cobnut tree and handed the boy root meat.

The boy was eager to try new forest fruits and nuts, and now roots. He lay and felt the damp floor under his back and arms and legs and chewed. "I like rubyroot."

"I have not seen it this close to the sea. I hear the Men have rubyroot and yuca and ginger and arrowroot in a large patch near their home."

"You seek the Men, Dahlia?" the boy asked through his chewing.

"I do. Why have you come to the forest?"

"I look for the sea man. I want to know the medicine for war-harm."

"We look for the same," Dahlia said. "The Men have found the sea man, but he remains to be caught and understood. The Men pursue him too."

The boy liked Dahlia. He did not want to go away from his new friend and was hesitant to express doubt in the sneaking and hunting of the white shimmer. He did not tell Dahlia about his dream or what he learned sitting with his father. The boy only knew the sea man was of the island and he enjoyed walking with Dahlia.

"May I walk with you?"

"My hope fulfilled!" Dahlia said.

Dahlia wrapped rubyroot and kiwis and cobnuts in a palm. The boy, less experienced in the forest, imitated. He trusted Dahlia's experience. The boy wondered if it necessary, though; he thought the forest would provide. His mother gathered fresh fruits and ripe nuts each sunrise, never taking more than they would enjoy.

Why should I, only in the forest for a few sunrises and sunsets, know what lies further? We may not find sweeter rubyroot! he thought.

"Come, friend."

As the pair walked, the boy thought of his dream from long ago, his first time in the forest. He wondered about his dream friends, if he would speak to them again and if he might ever take journey with them. He remembered washing his face and hands in that stream where he met the man with hair like his father's and the white bird. That stream, he remembered now and for the first time, glowed. Perhaps it was the sun within his dream? He thought not. This glow was from within; it perfumed the stream and enlightened the shadows of the canopy. I'd like to see that again, he thought. Dahlia would enjoy my dream friends.

"How will we find the Men?" the boy asked his friend.

"The opposite side of the island to your sturdy wood home, the sand turns to forest floor, and the forest floor turns to black, soft stone. This black, soft stone climbs and climbs into a blue rock mountain. On the opposite side of the blue rock mountain from the sea, palms as tall as three fill an orchard of smooth, fine sand."

"Sand, in the forest?" the boy asked.

"An orchard of palms as tall as three and smooth, fine sand. The orchard of palms lasts in three directions. In the fourth, and between the orchard and the gold sand of the sea, a blue rock mountain climbs," Dahlia said.

The boy was mesmerized. He pictured these places and yearned to fly over them with the green and purple birds with bright orange feet. He wondered if this far gold sand hosted small claws and who might live there.

"There live people in the palm orchard," Dahlia went on. "As you from the sea, from the gold sand, people come from the palms as tall as three, too."

People of the palms as tall as three? The boy smiled.

"These sleep under the emerald light. They shelter under the sky. They grow Punica and lemons on the side of the blue rock mountain." Dahlia laughed. "My mother told me the orchard is so large palms as tall as three on one side harvest five hundred sunrises before palms as tall as three on the farther side!"

The two stopped walking and each sat on a boulder, the boy on a mossed brown and Dahlia on a slate shelf. They faced and spoke. A patch of rubyroot grew between them, delighting the pair.

"Why go there?" the boy asked.

"The people of the palms as tall as three and smooth, fine sand know where the Men keep home," Dahlia said. "This also my mother told me, when I was small and dreamt of the white shimmer."

"You, too, dreamt of the white shimmer?" the boy asked.

Dahlia looked at the boy with a proud chin. "I was called by adventure and purpose into the forest; I had a dream about running after the white shimmer. I near touched it, I think. I ran after it with the Men."

"I have seen this dream."

Dahlia was silent for a time as they sat.

"Was there a white bird in your dream?" the boy asked.

"No bird. A shimmer."

37

Curious, the boy thought.

"Dahlia, what do you know of the Men?"

"I am nervous to meet them," Dahlia admitted.

"Why? I know little. My brother is there, but I have not seen him for many sunrises and sunsets. I remember little of him."

"I heard they are wary of those new," Dahlia said.

This the boy feared. Would his brother be glad to see him?

"They exist in constant pursuit and contemplation of the white shimmer. This path I fear. I wandered for a time and lived with those three creatures for a time, without structure or contemplation or pursuit. My pursuit is pursuit itself. I want to know the sneaking and hunting, but I fear I will not." Dahlia felt wandering in conversation and paused.

The boy felt Dahlia's nervous words and handed his companion meat from his rubyroot of the previous patch. They ate together in silence for a time, as two friends at odds might.

That first night of their journey, the pair rested on these boulders. Loos of night birds kept the forest air warm and the two slept well.

The boy dreamt:

He and Dahlia fought through vines, dense and thick forest, following a scent the boy never smelled. He asked had Dahlia smelled it. His friend had not. The forest turned grey; a fine black and white dust covered the floor.

The boy smelled and tasted the dust. It was foul, like no smell or taste he had smelled or tasted. He knew it did not belong here in the forest. The sound of the forest was plagued by this dust; birds and creatures and rocks and palms and wind and stream and floor toiled for breath. All were sick with grey and dust. The closer he and Dahlia came to the source of the scent, the more drowned the forest became.

"Dahlia." The boy gasped. "Have we left the forest?"

Dahlia turned to face him; his companion's face was grey—not in dust, but in skin.

"Friend!" Dahlia said, as one woken from a dream.

The boy repeated.

"The white shimmer waits; the Men say so!"

"The white shimmer entertains; it is not to catch. It does not serve." The boy's mouth filled with dust.

Dahlia laughed and continued moving through vines and dense, thick forest. "Come."

The boy could not contest or stop his legs. The grey enveloped him; the dust covered him. His eyes and nose and ears and tongue burned. His hands and feet were weightless and without sensation.

Coming, at last, through the vines, the boy and Dahlia saw a white shadow, one shimmering in the grey, surrounded by grey trees and falling dust. The white shimmer stood in stark contrast to the grey forest, and from its head rose a spiraled column of black cloud.

Dahlia prostrated, with dozens of the Men, facing the white shimmer.

It captivated the boy. He went to prostrate too. He saw, within the white shimmer, the sea man, as did each of the other prostrating.

The boy looked at the white shimmer and asked, "What is war-harm? And how can I prevent it?"

A white bird landed on the back of one prostrated near the boy.

"My friend," the boy said.

The white bird, resting in stark contrast to the grey and the white shimmer, whispered a word, one the boy knew not.

Nine

THE BOY WOKE as Dahlia crashed through some low trees, arms clutching a heap of round, orange fruits.

The boy looked about the forest. It had only been a dream. The grey was of his mind. He did not wonder what the white bird whispered because he forgot it had whispered. He remembered the vines and the grey and the dust and the prostrated Men and the white shimmer; he did not remember the bird.

The boy smiled and breathed with excitement for his company and their adventure.

The two enjoyed rubyroot and the round, orange fruits. They smiled as they ate, sometimes at each other and sometimes at the stream and sometimes at the rubyroot and round, orange fruits.

A mantis crept the mossed brown boulder and the boy offered it rubyroot, remembering his wise father's words: "The sea man is of the island and all things on the island." The mantis crept.

"Dahlia," the boy said.

"I'm here."

"Why do the Men—why do we—sneak and hunt after the white shimmer? Do you know?"

"The sea man came into the forest after three emerald nights, after his wife and boy were lost, after he smiled at the sea. His spirit, with the medicine for war-harm, lives in the white shimmer. If caught, he might tell us of war-harm, what he learned on the sea." Dahlia knew well.

"Would the sea man not want us to know of war-harm? Why would he hide for us, for the Men, to pursue?"

Dahlia took an orange fruit and looked down.

The boy did not mean to trap his friend; his interest was sincere. He watched as the orange fruit disappeared and pondered the question too.

"The sea man and the white shimmer are one," Dahlia said. The boy withheld his wise father's words, fearing offense and distrust. He, too, wanted to meet the Men. "The white shimmer holds the secrets learned when he left and walked upon the sea, those of war-harm. If he gave the Men answers without strife, his secrets would be abused. Our pursuit of the white shimmer is his walking onto the sea. It may also, my father told me, take a special one to approach and capture the white shimmer."

"A special one?" He blushed and imagined himself the approacher and captor; the excitement of the Men surrounded him. One new revealing the secrets of war-harm, of the sea man! His cheeks went red. Dahlia would laugh, he was sure. He would be invited to return to the orchard of the palms as tall as three and smooth, fine sand. He would climb the blue rock mountain with his friend. He would go home and tell his father and mother the secrets of war-harm. Father, he'd say, the sea man was in the white shimmer! I approached without rejection and caught the sea man. He saw his wise father's eyes fill with tears, like on the day his brother left. His father would be glad. He, his brother, his father, and his mother would sit for a meal of fresh fruits and ripe nuts and rubyroot. Dahlia would join them.

"What will happen when the special one approaches and captures the white shimmer?" The boy, lost in fantasy, urged his friend forward.

"Do you think yourself this special one?" Dahlia asked.

"You have not thought of it yourself?"

"Yes," Dahlia said.

"I have too, now."

"I do not know what will happen when the special one approaches and captures the white shimmer. My father told me the special one would go away with the sea man for many sunrises and sunsets and the sea man would teach the special one the medicine for war-harm and what he learned on the sea."

A chill crawled the boy's spine. Could this be the journey his dream friends spoke of? Am I this special one? he thought.

"What do you think is war-harm, Dahlia?"

"I think it is an enemy, here or far, that wants to have our island. Purpose," Dahlia ventured past the boy's question, "is finding that which prevents war-harm from reaching us. One will find it, maybe this special one. Adventure brought us here. Adventure is why children want to join the Men before they know purpose."

The boy stayed fascinated in this conversation and thought Dahlia wise. He thought to his father's words and to his dream. Do dreams mean what occurs or do they go with our preoccupations? The boy did not know.

"If you are not this special one?" the boy asked.

Dahlia frowned and said, "I will look forward to hearing what the special one learns from the sea man. You and I may be no more special than the Men who practice sneaking and hunting now."

The boy frowned too. He thought he should not have asked this.

"We are special to each other. You have given me grand adventure and I have given you"—the boy tossed Dahlia a piece of rubyroot—"the sweetest rubyroot I have had."

"Grand adventure?"

"I might wander without purpose and without knowing how to find the medicine for war-harm had the three figures not brought me to you and had we not escaped and had you not welcomed me to your journey."

Dahlia chewed the rubyroot. "I believe this rubyroot is sweet. Thank you."

They each smiled and the boy pondered this special one.

That day the two set out for the orchard of palms as tall as three and the smooth, fine sand.

Now the boy still did not know his path. He thought Dahlia was enjoyable company and fascinating in conversation, but he did not forget the words of his wise father. He pondered, as the two walked along the cool stream, the best explanation of the sea man.

Could my wise father who has seen so many sunrises and sunsets be wrong about the Men of the forest? Is it possible the white shimmer charms and does not serve? The boy believed the sea man was of the island and all things on the island. What of the white shimmer? He worried of being charmed against his father's warning.

He groaned beneath the sounds of the forest and thought hard on everything.

Had I not followed the white bird into the forest, might my wise father have taught—in easy words—the story of the sea man and the medicine for war-harm? he wondered.

The boy chose—moving forward—to take no lesson without his father's words in mind.

This choosing calmed the boy's thoughts and allowed him to enjoy Dahlia's company and the forest. He entertained thoughts of adventure as the two walked.

"Dahlia, how do you know the people of the palms as tall as three know where the Men keep home?" the boy asked after some time of adventure thought.

"I already told you this: my mother told me when I was small, when I dreamt of the white shimmer," his friend replied. The boy felt embarrassed and Dahlia turned and saw this. "Do not be embarrassed."

"I forgot we spoke of this before," the boy said.

"And I have forgotten you spoke of it again," Dahlia said.

"Do you know what they will tell us?"

"I hope they tell us where the Men keep home and how you and I might go there."

"Did your mother say how they are?" the boy asked. "Your mother said they sleep under the emerald light and shelter under the sky and they grow Punica and lemons on the side of the blue rock mountain. Your mother said the orchard is so large, palms as tall as three on one side harvest five hundred sunrises before palms as tall as three on the farther side. How are they?"

"My mother told me—when I was small—the people of the palms as tall as three revere the orchard and guard its beauty from any who come against."

"We do not come against," the boy said.

"These do not believe in the sneaking and the hunting. Small people of the palms as tall as three who leave do not return," Dahlia said.

"They do not believe in the sneaking and the hunting?"

"They believe the spirit of the sea man is of the island and all things on the island. They do not believe the white shimmer real. It is an illusion, they say."

"What, then, of war-harm?" the boy asked.

"I do not know," Dahlia said. "I cannot believe an island with no white shimmer and without sneaking and hunting will learn the medicine for war-harm. Where would the island learn it if not from the sea man in the white shimmer?"

The boy did not know. "I look to enjoy meeting the people of the palms as tall as three."

"I hope they will tell us where the Men keep home," Dahlia said.

"If they do not?"

"I hope they will."

When sunset came and passed, the boy and Dahlia rested under the forest canopy, the boy between two felled palms, mossed and rot, and Dahlia on the soft streambank.

The boy dreamt:

He and Dahlia sat near a lake made of the sun. The sun lake, however, did not give warmth, and it did not make the boy smile. It made his skin hot and his eyes narrow. The boy looked to Dahlia and saw his friend smiling in the heat of the sun lake with eyes wide.

"Dahlia looks happy," he said aloud. Dahlia's eyes stayed in the heat.

Two turtles and a white bird sat on a log suspended over the sun lake. The white bird rested in stark contrast to the heat. The sun lake is too hot for those, the boy thought as he watched from the shore.

From the heat of the sun lake rose a figure, a man made of fire. This man made of fire sat on the log and whispered to one turtle; the word rose and filled the air as the heat, but the boy knew not what it meant. The turtle slid into the fire with no regard.

Dahlia, still seated with the boy, laughed at nothing or the turtle's slide. Which, the boy knew not.

The man made of fire, a charred coal smile spread wide on his red face, sank back into the lake. The white bird, resting in stark contrast to the heat, whispered to the other turtle. Again, the word rose. This time, it relieved the heat of the sun lake in the air; again, the boy knew not what it meant.

With this word, the place where the boy and Dahlia sat came alive. It was black dirt, dry by the heat of the sun lake. Then hundreds of sprouts came. All around the boy and Dahlia, green and blue and orange and purple blossoms painted the floor. A palm grew. And another. Soon the two sat beneath a lemon tree. Dahlia sang and the boy was paralyzed with joy. The barren shore bloomed. Vines tangled and small turtles climbed from the dirt, and lemons and Punica and limes perfumed the air.

This turtle, the one which received the word of the white bird, put one turtle foot into the sun lake. The turtle's eyes closed, and it smiled. The boy had never seen a turtle smile. It smiled not as the man made of fire smiled; this smile was of relief instead of opportunity. The turtle appeared satisfied, filled as the shore was now filled, black dirt replaced with blossom and perfume. The turtle, still with a smile, let out the same word the bird whispered. The boy still knew not the word. When the turtle finished its word, the lake of fire, that hot and wicked sun lake, cooled. The flames dispersed from the turtle foot on until the whole lake was quenched deep blue. The first turtle, which received the word from the man made of fire, climbed back onto the log. The turtle was unhurt. The white bird looked at the boy sitting on the blossomed and perfumed shore. It flew away.

Ten

THE ORCHARD OF PALMS as tall as three and smooth, fine sand reminded the boy of a field of grass he saw once in a reef of coral. The orchard broke from the forest with such contrast of color and air the boy forgot, upon leaving the forest, he ever was in the forest. The palms as tall as three fashioned rows farther than any eye could see forward and running parallel to the forest. Beyond, rising into the immense blue sky and near the sun, mountains of deep blue rock guarded the orchard from the sea. The boy imagined—he could not see far through the orchard—lemon and Punica trees growing in the hills, as Dahlia told him.

The boy turned and looked where the black forest floor turned to white sand and where low plants, prickly or smooth or long or short, stopped growing to reveal how tall these palms were. Insect and forest bird and tree creature hummed on one side; on the other, the air was still and hot.

The boy looked at Dahlia. His friend's arms were stretched wide and the hands formed fans. Dahlia spun in the hot air as one dancing might. The boy thought Dahlia like a sunrise fish.

"I enjoy this orchard," Dahlia said, still spinning with outstretched arms.

The boy looked now into the orchard itself. Coming from the forest, the boy thought the orchard a still and hot contrast to the forest, like a field of grass surrounded by a coral reef and sea creatures. Now the boy saw the orchard as a forest of its own.

The white sand was shaded forever; only where he and Dahlia stood, or spun, near the forest was it exposed to the sun.

The boy stepped into the shade of the first row of palms. He imagined climbing one and thought he might not reach the top. Even those tallest palms he climbed when he was small came less than halfway to the tops of these. The branches were thick and the deepest green the boy had seen. He saw nuts, ripe and otherwise, larger than the largest ripe nuts he enjoyed with his father and mother. He thought one might feed ten. He wondered how the people of the palms as tall as three gathered these.

Even shaded from the sun, the air was still and hot. The boy shifted his feet in the warm sand and raised his eyes to the sun-glowed palm branches. He smiled and thanked the sun for warmth.

The boy stepped into the next row and thought the place beautiful and mysterious. The sea teemed with life and the forest vibrated with energy; this place wondered of itself. The still and hot air and the palms as tall as three and smooth, fine sand each wondered about the other; this wonder from each was passed on to the boy and Dahlia as they stood, or spun.

"We ought to not wander far without water," the boy said. The stream the two followed to this place disappeared into a wet rock formation. The boy thought it might travel under the orchard to the sea. "There may be no water in the orchard."

Dahlia agreed and the two sat for a time next to the disappearing stream, forced under the sand by the orchard's hot breath. Under the forest canopy, the air was cooler. Each had salt dry on their faces.

"Do you know where the people of the palms as tall as three keep home in the orchard?" the boy asked.

"No. Only that they live here and grow Punica and lemons on the side of the blue rock mountain."

"Mountains," the boy said.

"Is more than one peak more than one mountain?" Dahlia asked.

"I do not know."

The two had a few cobnuts and a kiwi and two limes and they resolved to spend the night there, where the dry sand pulled with some ancient desire on the wet air of the forest. Before sunrise, they would wander into the orchard.

The boy decided the air in the orchard was like the sea air, though without wind, and he lay where the sand was warm between the tree line of the forest and the first row of palms as tall as three. He thought of his father and mother and wondered if either had been to this place. He scooped sand into each hand and let it run through his fingers, imagining his father doing the same. He wondered if his brother came here on his journey to the Men. The boy sat and saw his brother standing on the white sand, marveling at the palms.

What sort of people live here? he wondered. He hoped they would tell him and Dahlia where the Men kept home. If they did not, the boy thought, he might stay here and live with them. He smiled at such a thought. No, he would return to the gold sand and their sturdy wood home and spend his time with his father and mother. Dahlia might join him. Dahlia was adventurous and curious; his father would like his new friend.

The boy's mind wandered to his dream friends. He thought of the white bird flying from the sand into the forest and hiding him and Dahlia from the wailing figure and visiting his strange dreams. Was this white bird only an illusion, as the white shimmer is said to be for the Men? He thought to ask Dahlia about seeing the white bird that night the wailing creature came, but Dahlia rested, and the boy thought to not wake his friend. He resolved to speak to the white bird if he saw it again. The man with hair like his father's said the bird would speak back. Not to those paralyzed with curiosity and surprise and fear, the boy thought. He laughed and said, "I will speak to the white bird when I see him again."

The day left and sunset approached. The boy knew sunset fell on the other side of the island; he often watched it with his father and mother. Sitting in the sand with the evening rolling of sea foam, they would enjoy kiwis as the sun crawled below the horizon.

He expected little and thought the sun would fall over the forest and leave the pair in some strange meeting place of two darknesses. He and Dahlia walked into the orchard as the day's light faded, curious for the new place.

The sun lowered and its light skirted the tops of the palms as tall as three. A green hue filled the orchard, and the white sand appeared as soft and new moss. In the distance, the blue rock mountains lit the evening sky with a show of swirling beams of purple. The boy and Dahlia stood in green and purple awe.

The emerald light in the sky, rising above the orchard, turned to a deep blue, like a nighttime patch of Muscari blossoms near a trickling stream. Time crept slower, slower, and stood in still adoration.

The green hue and moss sand and swirling beams of purple and Muscari light in the sky created such wonder in the boy and Dahlia neither could contain laughter. Dahlia spun like earlier, and the boy touched the sand to remember it was sand and they were still in the orchard and not transported to the dream of a stranger.

The green hue and moss sand stayed even when the sun disappeared, as if trapped by the thick branches of the palms. When the swirling beams of purple vanished and the Muscari light in the sky returned to emerald, the green faded.

The two stood in the darkest night they had seen. The boy outstretched his hand and could not count his fingers. He lost sight of Dahlia. The boy blinked twice. And again. After a third blinking, the orchard came visible again. There was Dahlia, still spinning under the black palms.

"I could not see you," the boy said.

"Nor I, you."

"You must be dizzy with the spinning."

"I am not. The green hue and moss sand and swirling beams of purple and Muscari light in the sky balanced even while I spun. Earlier, the spinning made me dizzy. Now, it did not."

The two sat in the darkness of the orchard and pondered different courses.

The boy thought of Dahlia spinning and his dream friends and staying in this orchard forever and never finding the Men. Then of finding the Men and being the special one and finding his brother and returning home. What if I am the special one? the boy thought.

Dahlia thought of the Muscari light and hoped to see it again, of Muscari blossoms and the stream they walked to reach here, and of the people of the palms as tall as three. Dahlia wondered if, searching for the Men, they came against these. Then of the special one, the one who might approach the white shimmer. What if I am the special one? Dahlia thought.

The thoughts swirled in the darkness of the orchard. Neither spoke and neither cared to. The orchard's sunset gave their imaginations course to run and explore, free from the intrusion of conversation.

The boy wondered if there was depth to the sunset beyond its fading to uncertain memory. He thought there might be a way to feel it and know it after it left. The boy imagined his mother sitting near and remembered her fascination with smell and taste and sight and sound. She sat with him and took a kiwi and tasted it and laughed. Why do you laugh at the kiwi? the boy asked. Taste it, his mother said. The boy tasted and swallowed the kiwi and did not understand why his mother laughed. The kiwi turned into a shell and his mother put the shell to her ear and laughed and again the boy did not understand. The boy watched and marveled at her simple joy and still his thoughts swirled.

Dahlia broke the silent air: "Should we rest?"

The boy was near sleep when his friend asked. "Yes."

"Here?"

"Where then?" the boy asked. "I never want to leave the smooth, fine sand of this orchard."

"Until we learn of the Men," Dahlia said.

"Until we learn of the Men." The boy sighed and let sleep come.

Dahlia sat and looked at the emerald light in the sky, glowing through the still palms, and wondered why it was not so bright like the sun.

Eleven

THE AIR WAS HOT AND STILL when the two woke. The boy rubbed his sleep away and looked at his companion, curled on the cool, white sand, looking back at him.

"Had we dreamed?" the boy asked.

"I did not dream last night. Do you mean the moss sand and green hue and swirling beams of purple and Muscari light in the sky?" Dahlia asked.

"Yes."

"We saw them," Dahlia said.

The boy closed his eyes and saw it all again in still, pretty images, but he did not wonder or laugh. It was a fractured beauty that could not be held. He frowned and looked forward to sunset.

Dahlia washed in the cool stream where it disappeared from the edge of the forest. The boy sat and drank.

"We will walk the rows?" the boy asked.

"We will walk the rows to the blue rock mountain and hope to see a person of the palms as tall as three along the way," Dahlia said.

They set out into the rows of palms as tall as three. The pace was slow, and the morning air stayed still and hot. Dahlia, always eager, led and the boy followed. He tried to step in Dahlia's footprints because the sand was often soft and deep and made for hard walking. The boy marveled at the expanse of palms and thought it curious he had seen no other formation or life; no rock or stream or shrub or blossom or mantis or tree creature kept home in the orchard. The stillness and reverence of the place struck him. He wondered if Dahlia thought the orchard strange but did not ask; his friend had been in hard contemplation during their walk.

After some time and after walking a considerable distance (though neither the boy nor Dahlia could say how far they had come—they were now surrounded by palms as tall as three), the two stopped to rest. The boy thought Dahlia bored of the scene, and he felt bored too.

"We will need water soon," Dahlia said.

The boy nodded and felt the thirst and hunger of the two.

"I have seen only rows and smooth, fine sand," Dahlia said.

"I think I saw a bird once," the boy said. Dahlia smiled and leaned onto the base of a palm. The smile's corners climbed, showing even teeth as white as the sand.

"This place is beautiful. Beautiful and boring to walk," Dahlia said.

The boy looked around. Palms and a blue rock mountain still far in the distance. "We could have the nectar from a ripe nut."

Dahlia looked at a palm as tall as three. "I cannot make the climb."

The boy did the same. "I may. Let us continue and, when thirst calls stronger, I will make the climb."

The boy would not have to make the climb. A short time after his bravery, the two walked upon two small ones playing chase. They wound through the palms and laughed, kicking white sand in the warmth of the sun. One fell and the other laughed. The one who fell gave chase until the two were panting and laughing and covered in sand and warmth.

"Hello!" Dahlia said.

The two small ones smiled and walked to meet the boy and Dahlia.

"Enchanting sun day," one taller with skin as dark as a ripe nut said.

"An enchanting sun day," the other said, this one shorter with long hair and freckled, dark skin.

"Do you enjoy the warmth of the sun?" Dahlia asked.

"It leaves us panting and laughing and covered in sand and warmth. It makes a cool dip much cooler."

"You will take a dip?" Dahlia asked.

"In the cascade!" the taller said

"Where is the cascade?" Dahlia asked. The boy knew not what a cascade was but assumed it water from the conversation.

"It runs from the blue rock mountains through the center of our orchard on this enchanting sun day—it is an enchanting sun day—to the basin where we rest," the taller said.

"Are we near your basin?" Dahlia asked with a smile.

"Close enough!" the freckled said.

The small ones, one taller and the other freckled, led the boy and Dahlia parallel to the blue rock mountains and parallel to the forest toward the center of the orchard. The taller took Dahlia's hand and the freckled took the boy's. The small ones were less curious about the strangers than excited to share their orchard. "This palm is the first I climbed," one would say. The other would laugh and call it untrue. "Here is where I found a slithering creature," one would say. The other would shriek and the small ones would laugh and hop. "Here is where my mother found the largest ripe nut our orchard ever saw," one would claim. The small ones would talk about this nut and their mother and laugh and claim untrue or agree and shake the hand of the stranger and urge belief. And this went on, the boy laughing and playing and Dahlia daydreaming, laughing only when the daydream was broken by the taller one shaking the hand and urging belief.

Soon, and to the surprise and relief of the boy and Dahlia, the four reached a winding and weaving rocky stream. It bubbled and flowed and splashed, and the small ones washed the sand and warmth from their skin. The boy and Dahlia washed their faces and drank. The cascade was surrounded without end by palms. Its pink and grey rocks were large and smooth and created the bubbling and flowing and splashing.

"Your cascade is frigid," the boy said to the taller one.

"It is melt from the tops of the blue rock mountains," this one replied.

"Melt?" the boy asked.

The small ones laughed and splashed and went under the frigid water and came back and gasped and continued to laugh. The boy thought not to ask again.

Soon the small ones returned to the chasing and kicking white sand and panting and laughing.

"Will you take us to your home?" Dahlia asked.

"If we return now, Father will not allow us to leave again until sunset and sunrise," the freckled said.

"Follow the frigid!" the taller said as the two ran off, kicking white sand in the warmth of the sun.

The boy and Dahlia looked at each other, toward the blue rock mountains, and their eyes followed the cascade to where the small ones supposed a basin.

"Follow it where?" the boy asked.

"I do not know." Dahlia turned around and the small ones were gone.

"They grow lemons and Punica on the side of the blue rock mountains," the boy said.

"The small ones said they rested at the basin."

"Yes?" the boy asked.

"I am sure."

"The basin, then."

"I would taste a kiwi and rubyroot now," Dahlia said.

"I would taste a whole patch and enjoy it."

They laughed, and Dahlia hoped for kiwi and rubyroot at the basin and the boy hoped for sun chuara and cobnuts.

"Have you had sun chuara?" the boy asked Dahlia. The two walked along the cascade.

"No."

"I would like to show you sun chuara. I wonder if there will be any at the basin."

The two walked and spoke of sun chuara and other fresh fruits and which fruits went with which ripe nuts and different ways to enjoy fresh fruits and ripe nuts and now rubyroot. Dahlia spoke again of the Men and their yuca and ginger and arrowroot and wondered if the two would enjoy these. The boy did not know.

"We must see the basin soon," Dahlia said. "Those small ones cannot wander far."

"I hope," the boy said. Their conversation returned to fresh fruits and ripe nuts and now ripe roots.

Soon the cascade widened and widened and dropped steep. It descended the pink and grey rocks and rounded into an easy basin. Its size impressed the boy and Dahlia.

"This seems a lake," the boy said.

"This seems a sea," Dahlia said. The two stood atop a dune of sand, perched over the descending water, to look about.

The whole basin was surrounded by root patch of so many sorts they could not be counted. The patch grew on a wide and sloping black dirt bank.

"Rubyroot there. And what is that? Do you see the vines there? There *must* be ginger here."

He saw Dahlia's eyes wide. His friend looked struck with awe in hunger.

Outside this encompassing root patch stood low fruit and nut trees: Punica, lemon, cobnut, lime, chuara, blossoms, and more. Rare birds kept home in these spread trees and winged insects fluttered and buzzed, touring their oasis. When he came from the forest into the orchard, the boy felt he had never even been in the forest. Now, looking across this basin, he felt he had never been in the orchard.

On the far side of the basin, which the boy called a lake and Dahlia called a sea, past the encompassing root patch and low fruit and nut trees alive with birds and winged insects, was a clearing, the only in the orchard, the boy thought. He could not see through the low trees enough to understand the clearing, but he thought people moved about it. Dahlia thought so too.

"This is an enchanting sun day," the boy said with a laugh. He did not know why the small ones called the day sun day.

"Should we see the clearing?" Dahlia asked.

"I would taste these," the boy said, his eyes dancing from root to nut to fruit and back again to the roots of the patch.

"Maybe they will have us for a meal."

Dahlia walked, and the boy followed, frowning for their passing of curious and aromatic roots. His stomach frowned too.

Black dirt, like that of the forest floor, gave life to sprouts so green and so orange and so purple and so blue the boy thought again he was looking at a reef of coral. He said so, and Dahlia said he might need to experience things other than coral. The boy asked if Dahlia had seen coral. No.

"Perhaps they have a meal prepared. We might join," Dahlia said.

"We should sit and enjoy these." The boy's eyes begged the roots and sprouts to leap from the black dirt.

"We should meet those behind the fruit and nut trees before we enjoy their roots or ripe nuts or fresh fruits," Dahlia said.

They walked along the basin, and the boy thought it shallow across, unlike the sea or—even though he had not seen a lake— a lake. "You could walk across this basin," he said. If not for Dahlia's quick steps, he might have lain in the clear, still water and chewed on rubyroot or something new. He remembered the frigid cascade and shuddered.

Soon, the two reached the far side of the basin and ducked under a lemon tree into a small forest of ripe fruits. Dahlia again told the boy to hold his hunger. He knew.

They weaved through the trees. A buzzing in the boy's ear was a yellow fly and a tickle on his neck, a forest moth. He thought not of their sound but of their color and way of moving. He thought to when he ran with the green and purple birds with bright orange feet and his father said he might fly away with them.

"I might like to stay here and fly about." Dahlia did not hear him.

Passing a blue tree in full blossom and a bright green one, the boy and Dahlia poked through the low trees into the clearing.

People sat around one tree at the far end of the clearing, facing away from the boy and Dahlia. Quiet, happy conversation filled the space.

"This tree is special," the boy said.

"I do not know."

The conversation of these gathered broke apart and scattered until the clearing was silent in the still and hot air, heavy with the perfumes of fruits and blossoms. Large piles of lemon and Punica and lime waited for just attention near the group. The boy imagined this clearing a good place for a sturdy wood home. Perhaps he could build it of pink and grey stones from the cascade. He smiled. Forever he might live here with the black dirt and plenty of trees and the shallow basin. His eyes found the sun and he sighed, glad for this adventure with Dahlia.

"Shall we join?" Dahlia wondered aloud.

"Let's see," the boy said. And so the two waited to see.

From beyond the clearing and in front of those gathered, a tall man emerged. His hair was brown and long and his white robe, black along the bottom from dragging, shone brilliant in the sun. He spoke and passed lemons and lime and Punica to those gathered.

"They seem fair," Dahlia said. "Let's not see any more. Come."

Dahlia turned and saw the boy's mouth and eyes wide. He was struck silent in awe. Dahlia spoke again but he did not hear.

The man had long brown hair like the boy's father's and, resting on his shoulder, was a white bird.

Twelve

THE BOY WAS STRUCK SILENT by the man and the white bird. He did not hear what Dahlia said, though he saw his friend step forward and speak to him.

His dream friends were real, not an illusion of his mind. The white bird had been with him on the gold sand and had flown over the forest and had shown the boy and Dahlia to the safety of the crevice and had thrown the wailing figure into despair.

The boy's mind raced and tried to make sense of his journey. His fear grew and he squatted out of sight, wondering what they might think of him and what they might say. He thought the white bird might not speak to him in front of these gathered.

"Dahlia, wait," the boy said.

"Let's not see anymore; we should join the group. They seem fair," Dahlia said.

He could not find the words to make his friend stay with him and stammered as his eyes leapt from his dream friends to Dahlia's impatient and confused gaze.

"We ought to meet them," Dahlia said.

"This cannot be all the people of the palms as tall as three," the boy said. "Let's see if there are more. We might not know if we join this group and they do not enjoy us and they send us away."

The boy and Dahlia spoke on this matter, and the boy convinced his friend to wait in the line of fruit and nut trees and observe the gathering. Dahlia thought it strange to do and the boy thought how to explain his dream friends to Dahlia.

Dahlia watched the gathering with interest and the boy's thoughts wandered. Should he tell Dahlia? Should he say hello to his dream friends? What would they say? Could he still journey with them? Could Dahlia come? Would Dahlia come? The boy looked at Dahlia and thought his friend would not come on any journey with these unless it ended with the Men. Perhaps their journey led to the Men and this was the place he and Dahlia were meant to come! We should join, the boy thought. Then he thought again to wait and see what this gathering was about.

The gathering was conducted with little excitement. The man with hair like the boy's father spoke—though the boy and Dahlia could not hear—and the white bird rested on his shoulder. The man leaned forward and the bird leaned back. He let his arms wide and the bird adjusted and held. The man sat level with those gathered and the bird went with him.

"Curious, his bird," Dahlia said.

"Yes, curious," the boy replied.

When the man finished speaking, one stood and passed lemons and Punica and limes to the rest. A lime was offered to the bird, which tilted its head in apparent rejection (this amused the gathered).

All sat in a circle and held the fruits in hand and closed their eyes. All smiled. All rubbed the fruits in their hands and smiled again. This fruit-smiling continued until each of the gathered was tasting fruit and smiling; all eyes in the clearing were closed.

"Curious," Dahlia said.

The boy thought of his mother. She practiced the same fruit-smiling with limes and the orange fruits. He thought she would like the orchard of palms as tall as three and smooth, fine sand.

The fruit-smiling concluded, and the gathered formed a line and left the clearing on one side, making toward the basin behind the boy and Dahlia.

"They are going toward the cascade," the boy said.

The procession rounded the basin and stood near the quick water. The man, white bird gone from his shoulder, spoke, and two waded into the bubbling cascade. The two lowered their sunned heads into the water as the man spoke, then the procession continued in the direction from which the boy and Dahlia met the taller and the freckled.

The boy and Dahlia had climbed the dune of sand, rocky beneath, toward the cascade to watch the procession. Dahlia thought they ought to follow from a distance. The boy was to agree when the white bird landed on a pink stone, glistening wet at the edge of the falling water.

"My friend," the boy said, standing tall.

"It is a bird," Dahlia said with a curious glare.

"Did you not see this bird the night of the wailing figure? This bird led us to the waterfall and threw the wailing figure into despair," the boy said.

"I do not remember." Dahlia's face betrayed amusement.

"Do not follow the procession behind; join the procession," the bird said.

Dahlia laughed and wondered aloud if the bird spoke.

"I spoke," the bird said.

"I have never seen a bird speak man."

"I speak many languages and influence many men," the bird said. "Join the procession, boy and Dahlia."

The boy and Dahlia joined the procession as it made way along the cascade. They felt not as strangers; though most noticed their joining, none were curious about it.

The procession came to the place where the boy and Dahlia met the small ones and continued through the orchard of palms. As the procession passed, the small ones joined the boy and Dahlia at the back and again took their hands and told them about their mother, who was in the procession.

"Will you come to our home?" the taller asked.

"I know not where we will go," the boy said. "I would like to speak with the man in front who has the white bird as his friend."

"He is wise and kind," the freckled said.

The taller spoke to the freckled: "He does not like leavers."

"Leavers?" Dahlia asked.

"That is what I call those who go to find the Men. They are leavers," the taller said.

"He knows where the Men keep home?" Dahlia asked.

"Everyone knows where the Men keep home. We have one or two who become leavers every sunrise to join the Men."

"You know where the Men practice sneaking and hunting?" Dahlia asked the taller.

"Everyone knows. We do. You do not?"

"We have come from the forest to find the Men by the word of this orchard," Dahlia said.

"Any will tell you, if you ask. Though most will be sad for your leaving," the freckled said.

"The man who has the white bird as his friend does not like leavers?" the boy asked.

"He will be sad for your leaving our orchard," the taller said. "Though still, he would tell you where the Men practice sneaking and hunting."

"We will not go to the Men," the freckled said.

"Why?" the boy asked.

"The white shimmer does not serve. The white shimmer charms."

The boy looked at Dahlia, but his friend looked ahead, lost in thought. Knowing Dahlia did not hear what the freckled said, he continued the conversation, speaking clear.

"The white shimmer charms?" the boy asked, glancing at Dahlia.

"The Men see the sea man in the white shimmer, but my father told us"—the freckled looked at the taller—"the sea man is of the island and all things on the island so we come to the basin and—"

"I think we ought to ask the man with the white bird as his friend where the Men keep home," Dahlia said to the boy. "He smiles with the warmth of the sun. You two appreciate his company?"

The freckled and the taller confessed their appreciation of the man's company.

The procession continued along the cascade until the sun was low on the orchard. The blue rock mountains loomed ahead.

"We are near," the freckled said.

The boy and Dahlia saw strange homes. Layered and woven palms formed large mats stretched between four palms; each had room to stand and sit and enjoy a meal. The cascade, even and steady now, expanded and became quite a river. Each side of the river had these palm mats stretched about. The place, though old and fixed, felt nomadic. A bridge of big stones, pink and grey and smooth, lay across the river, connecting the palm mat homes on one side to those on the other.

"You sleep under the palm mats?" the boy asked the freckled.

The small ones laughed and tugged on their visitors' hands. The freckled said, "We sleep under the emerald light. We commune under our palm homes to sit and speak."

"You sleep on the sand under the emerald light?" Dahlia asked.

"Yes, on the white sand," the taller said.

The palm mats stretched forward to the blue rock mountains, and the boy marveled at how many people lived in the orchard. The whole place moved and danced in some structure of happy discipline. Men carried woven baskets of fresh fruits on their heads and small ones washed ripe roots in the river, guided by the patient hands of their smiling mothers. Others stood under palm mats and watched the procession. Some smiled and waved at the boy and Dahlia and others were unaware of the strangers. Still others looked and bowed their heads. The boy and Dahlia respected the bows with their own, though they knew not the meaning.

"Our mother will find our father, and all will prepare for sunset," the freckled said.

"We sleep after sunset," the taller said.

"After sunset is honored."

"Our father and mother would have you rest with us until sunrise," the taller said. "They would."

"Our father and mother enjoy travelers and strangers," the freckled said.

"We will come with you," Dahlia said.

"Where does the man with the white bird as his friend rest?" the boy asked.

"Albahr rests over the river. See there"—the taller pointed with the hand that did not hold Dahlia's—"Albahr rests there."

The boy's gaze followed the taller's arm and finger across the river to a palm mat stretched between four palms. It differed from the others. Fresh blossoms and vines draped the sides and three large containers stood near it. Ripe nuts of variety filled one; another held small orange and red fruits; the third held white dust, whiter than the sand underfoot.

"Albahr?"

The freckled and taller grinned at the boy.

"I will meet him at sunrise," he said. His eyes narrowed at the special palm mat, eager to see his dream friends.

"Albahr is fair and has a big smile," the freckled said, making a big smile in imitation.

The father and mother of the taller and freckled welcomed the boy and Dahlia and enjoyed the company of travelers and strangers. The boy spoke of the gold sand and his own father and mother and the small claws and the green and purple birds with bright orange feet. They blushed at his telling of their sturdy wood home and how they slept under its roof, not under the emerald light. Dahlia spoke of falling captive to the three figures, and the boy thought Dahlia a storyteller. They recounted escaping the three figures and walking the stream to the orchard, and Dahlia told the father and mother what was already known about the orchard and what surprised the travelers. The mother and father blushed and smiled and stole glances at each other and asked why the boy and Dahlia came to the orchard. The boy wanted to tell of meeting Albahr and the white bird which spoke man in a dream, but Dahlia spoke first (and Dahlia did not know of his dreams, so he thought it best to not say).

"We came into the forest and walked the stream together and came to this place because we seek the Men. We want to join the Men in the sneaking and hunting."

"Many have left our orchard for the same," the father said.

"What do you know of the Men?" the boy asked.

"Little. Those who leave do not return," he said. The boy thought this a sign of good for the Men. If the pursuit was in vain, most would return.

"Do you know where the Men keep home?" Dahlia asked. "We would rest here for one or two sunsets before setting to find them."

"The Men," the father said, "sneak and hunt in the forest, from which we are now far, beyond the basin. If you see the forest from the basin, the stream you came from would be on the right. Do you understand?"

The boy and Dahlia both understood.

"To find the Men, you would head straight to the forest and turn away from your stream. You would walk along the forest, away from your stream and away from the basin, until you came to a rubyroot patch at the head of a path. This path the Men keep. It is lined with felled palms and runs to where the Men keep home."

"How is the journey?" Dahlia asked.

"The air is still and hot in the mornings until the forest. Two sunsets and three sunrises to the rubyroot patch and one day on the path lined with felled palms."

Dahlia expressed thanks. With the small ones now chasing along the river, the boy and Dahlia joined the father and mother on the white sand to wait for the green hue and moss sand and swirling beams of purple and Muscari light in the sky.

Dahlia and the boy sat a short distance from the mother and father and spoke of the Men and the journey and the curious blushes and smiles and glances of their hosts. The boy thought they might hear more of the Men while they rested among the people of the palms as tall as three, but Dahlia wanted to continue as soon as after two sunrises. The boy wondered if Dahlia thought to be the special one.

"I would like to sit with this Albahr. Do you not want to hear more of the white bird which spoke man?" the boy asked his friend.

"I would like to learn from the Men. Do you not want to learn of the white shimmer and the sea man?" Dahlia asked.

The boy saw now Dahlia drew no line between the sea man and Albahr and the white bird which spoke man. It may be my fault, the boy thought, for not telling Dahlia sooner of my dreams and my father's words. He thought to explain it all the next day, though even to him this line of connection remained a mystery.

The sun made toward the tops of the palms.

Even washed in it each night, the people of the palms as tall as three awed at the sunset. Why did these—he looked about at the people seated on the moss sand—think the sneaking and hunting in vain? For the same as his father? The boy thought Albahr would have the answer and set to speak with him at sunrise.

The whole people of the palms as tall as three lay on the white sand under the emerald light and the boy wondered if they ever tired of seeing the same sky and each other.

Thirteen

THE SUNRISE brought the orchard to life at once.

All was like the day before: men carried woven baskets of fresh fruits on their heads and small ones washed ripe roots in the river, guided by the patient hands of their smiling mothers. Others stood under palm mats and watched those going about. People smiled and waved at each other and passed the boy and Dahlia with little curiosity. Still others bowed their heads and neither the boy nor Dahlia knew what this meant.

The small ones told Dahlia of some preparing to find the Men. Dahlia went at sunrise while the boy went to find Albahr and the white bird.

The boy walked around palm mats and stepped aside for those carrying baskets and saw how roots could be washed. He walked along the river and saw in its clear water yellow fish and blue fish and small claws and shells. He thought the river pretty and wondered if there were reefs to explore in it.

From where he stood on the side of the river, he thought he could see the water climbing and climbing away to the blue rock mountains, far away beyond the great bask of palm mats. He could not see far through the heat though, and wondered it an illusion. So he closed his eyes and imagined this river climbing into the blue rock mountains, but he did not know what sort of trees grew there or if there were people or what sorts of birds he might see.

"I would see the blue rock mountains," he said. He smiled and narrowed his eyes at the distant peaks, soft with the morning sun.

The boy looked toward the forest, but the river turned to a quick cascade and disappeared before he could see it end in the basin; he only saw the orchard. But the boy, having walked here, closed his eyes and felt the still and hot air of this place and remembered walking along the cascade and the basin and the root patch and the fruit and nut trees and the happy clearing where Albahr and the white bird came alive.

He crossed the bridge and made to the palm mat stretched and adorned with fresh blossoms and vines. Albahr stood near, speaking to another.

The boy waited.

When the conversation finished, Albahr came and stood before the boy.

"We have met?" the boy asked.

"You know as well as I."

"Your name is Albahr?" the boy asked.

The man laughed and said, "Call me Albahr."

The boy thought it a strange time to laugh. "Albahr, how did you come into my dream long ago? And how does your bird speak man, and why was he near through my journey?"

"You seek the Men? To learn of the sneaking and hunting?" Albahr asked.

"Yes. Dahlia and I."

"Then your journey is not ours, and I was wrong to come to your dream and my bird was wrong to stay near through your journey."

The boy's eyes narrowed. "I am not, then, to find the Men and sneak and hunt?"

"I cannot say where you are to," Albahr said, peeling an orange fruit with his slow hands.

"What of the journey you spoke of in my dream?" the boy asked. "You said we would take a journey together, and I asked about this journey and you told me to rest. Is the journey not to the Men and the sneaking and hunting?"

"Boy," Albahr said, "Dahlia will go to the Men without thought. You will go to the Men with thought. The subject of these thoughts I cannot see. It is your decision."

"I would take journey with you if you would speak plain."

"To take journey with me and the white bird, I will ask you a question."

"I will answer your question," the boy said.

"The question is this: is it best to love yourself, others, or our island?"

The boy's feet gripped the sand and he thought of each. Albahr placed both hands behind his back, holding the orange rind, and looked at the boy with soft eyes.

Himself? The boy loved himself. He thought himself adventurous. He loved his strength and his climbing and his swimming. He loved his patience in sitting with his father and watching his mother and his mind for following his dreams and the white bird. He loved himself for enjoying fresh fruits and ripe nuts and new roots and for Dahlia's enjoyment of his company.

Others? The boy loved others. He loved his father and mother for molding his body for strength and climbing and swimming and for allowing him to sit with them and watch them and learn from them. He loved his mother for her singing and her smile and her eyes, and he loved his father for his wisdom and wit. He loved Dahlia for company and laughter and discussion and for escaping the three figures. The boy loved the people of the palms as tall as three for their unbidden joy and for their lives.

The island? Without the gold sand and tall palms and the sea and reefs, the boy would have no strength or climbing or swimming to practice. He would have no place to sit with his father and watch his mother. They would share no kiwis or sun chuara. He would imagine no adventures with the green and purple birds with bright orange feet. He might never feel the warmth of the sunrise fish. The boy would have no sitting place to listen to his mother's song and he would not have dreamt and met Albahr and the white bird. There would be no forest and he would not have met Dahlia or escaped the three figures. The boy would have never come to the orchard of palms as tall as three and smooth, fine sand because such would not exist.

The boy thought hard, and Albahr's hands stayed behind and his eyes stayed soft.

The boy thought of his wise father and how he might answer this question. As surf enveloping one who wades into the sea, a strange yearning overcame the boy.

He saw himself on the gold sand the day his father taught him the truth of the sea man. The boy had asked of the medicine for war-harm and where he could find the sea man's smile if not in the white shimmer.

That day his father said to him: "Always remember: the sea man is the sand and the palms and the rocks and sea moss and fresh fruits and ripe nuts and green and purple birds with bright orange feet and small claws and the air and the sky and the water. He is the forest deer and night birds and tree creatures. He is you and me."

He smiled for his young self, lost in his father's careful words. Did he know I would come to this place? the boy thought. He looked about and knew his father had been to the orchard of palms as tall as three and smooth, fine sand.

The boy looked at Albahr, his dream friend with the soft smile, and said, "To love myself is to love others and to love the island. To love others is to love myself and to love the island. To love the island is to love others and to love myself. One cannot love one without the others. I cannot answer your question."

His heart raced for the indecorous taste of his words. His eyes went to the floor and he shifted about, worried for offense.

"You have answered it," Albahr said. "You have answered what many have failed to answer."

"You have asked others?"

"Many. Some answered and finished the journey. Some answered and left the journey. Many did not answer," Albahr said.

"I would like Dahlia to come on the journey," the boy said.

"Dahlia will not answer this question."

"I will explain it."

"Dahlia's mind is with the Men. Soon, Dahlia will join the Men and practice the sneaking and hunting."

"When will we journey? I will speak with Dahlia."

"You love Dahlia. Dahlia thinks to be the special one of the white shimmer." Albahr sighed. "Dahlia loves the white shimmer."

The boy was hurt at the thought and resolved to speak with Dahlia.

"Where is the journey?" the boy asked. "Will we go to the blue rock mountains? To the sand across these? Off to solitude in the deep orchard of palms as tall as three?"

"The journey is of the mind. We will where the experience is right," Albahr said.

"Which experience?" the boy asked.

"It is a song. At times it is at the basin. Other times the song is clearest near the cascade. The song is clear and wondrous in the forest and blue rock mountains and the sand across each of these. Boy, the journey we take is of the mind. You will know war-harm and you will know the sea man's smile."

The boy swallowed hard and nodded. He looked back across the river, hoping for a glance of Dahlia. His eyes came to Albahr's and he nodded again.

"You have answered the question; we will go."

Albahr tilted his head back in the still, hot air. The boy followed his eyes and saw, circling above, the white bird which spoke man. It circled lower and lower and came to rest on Albahr's shoulder.

"Hello," the boy said to the white bird.

"We three are together again." Its voice was gentle and stern. Now, speaking to Albahr: "The cascade."

"Boy," Albahr said, "take fresh fruits and come. Ready your eyes and ears, your tongue and hands, your breath and mind."

Sitting on a wide and pink stone across the river, Dahlia frowned at the boy's new companionship. A jealous sigh fell into the river and Dahlia wondered if the towering palms—as old as the island itself—could taste impatience.

Fourteen

THE BOY AND ALBAHR sat near the cascade, away from any palm mats, and the white bird rested on Albahr's shoulder. The boy shifted in the sand as one about to receive a gift and his toes danced with excitement. Albahr sat like stone, and for some time, his eyes were closed and the bird looked at the boy. With its black eyes, the boy could not tell if the bird's look was gentle or excited or cautious.

After a time, Albahr spoke: "The medicine for war-harm, boy, cannot be learned. It must be experienced. It is that which moors man to the island and men to each other. It is the song of which I spoke. Close your eyes and repeat these words in your mind."

The boy did as told and found the words easy to remember. Albahr was again still for a time. The white bird did its look.

"This song you cannot learn has a name," Albahr said before, again, going still for a time. The boy closed, and kept closed, his eyes.

The boy shifted in the sand with his eyes closed and still his toes danced with excitement. He turned over each of Albahr's sentences, looking for clues or foresight. The boy understood not where the lesson might end, and its pace surged his excitement.

"You knew it not, but this song has danced around you. You did not join, but it was there."

The boy's eyes stayed closed and he looked for clues.

"The song of the sea. The song of the reef. The song of the forest," Albahr said. "Think of the forest, boy."

The boy thought of the forest. He saw green and brown and moss and stone and stream and vine and many palms and a cobnut tree. He told Albahr this.

"And now the reef."

The boy thought of the reef. He saw sunrise fish and blue and green coral and now a fish that reminded him of the swirling beams of purple from the sunset in the orchard when it swam in circles. The boy saw tangled grass and sea claws and sponges and mushrooms and more coral and he smiled, sitting with Albahr and the white bird. He told Albahr what he saw.

"And now the sea, the gold sand from which you came," Albahr said.

The boy pictured green and purple birds with bright orange feet and small claws practicing their own sneaking and hunting by the emerald light. He thought of climbing palms and running over the gold sand and lying in the sun and feeling the warmth under his skin. The boy felt this warmth now, too, and expressed thanks. He imagined sitting with his wise father and watching his mother. He thought of his mother's song that lulled the boy to dream on their sitting place and he thought of their meals at sunset and kiwis and ripe nuts and sun chuara. The boy laughed with closed eyes and again told Albahr what he saw.

A soft breeze—the last breath of some strong wind pulled down from the blue rock mountains—shifted the still, hot air, and Albahr smiled without spectator.

"How do you enjoy the taste of the breeze?" he asked.

The boy opened his eyes and felt the still, hot air shift; the breeze danced across his skin. He breathed in, opened his mouth, and felt the breeze on his tongue. "The taste of the breeze?"

"Close your eyes," Albahr said, "and be gentle with the breeze. Let it fill your nose first."

The boy allowed the breeze to fill his nose and he was gentle with it. He held it captive in his nose, afraid to disappoint.

"Now, let it pass to your ears and open your mouth."

The boy thought it curious to allow a breeze to pass through one's nose to one's ears, but he did. He opened his mouth.

"Be gentle, boy," Albahr said. "Let the breeze whisper in your mouth. It touches the tongue, now the roof and the cheeks, and now you feel it on your throat. It is kind."

The boy was as gentle as the breeze itself and he allowed the breeze to whisper in his mouth. He felt the breeze touch his tongue and roof and cheeks and throat.

"Punica and lemons; young palms and fine sand and cool stream. Old and blue rock," Albahr said.

The boy felt the breeze in his nose and it passed to his ears and his mouth was filled with it. Punica and lemons and young palms and fine sand and frigid water and some strange stone: it whispered about his mouth, gentle and easy and pleasant. He tasted salt from a distant sea, hiding behind the proud blue rock mountains. A strange perfume of trees and rain came, passing from his nose to his ears, and filling his mouth with a curious thirst. He opened his eyes, unsure if he still sat in the orchard. He closed his eyes and smiled, searching again for that breeze.

Albahr saw the boy smile and close his eyes. "You have been given the Joy of Senses."

The still, hot air of the orchard parched the breeze. The boy watched this happen with his eyes closed: sand and ripe nuts, palms stretched and sunned, melted together in his nose. As they passed to his ears and he opened his mouth, the orchard felt familiar.

"The taste of the breeze is the medicine for war-harm?" the boy asked, squinting his eyes open.

"The taste of the breeze is one song in the Joy of Senses. Every palm and rock and grain of sand and lemon and kiwi and cobnut carries its own. The sea and reefs and the forest each have a song. Boy, you have experienced one song in the Joy of Senses," Albahr said. "Each song is unique. Some are of sight, others sound, others smell and taste, and others touch. Some come through the nose first, then the mouth. Others sing to the ear and after, dance across the tongue. The eyes will find a song, only to have it passed between the hands.

"Be gentle with smells and tastes. Appreciate the individual notes of their character without passing judgement. Let the notes build and consume your place."

Both the boy and Albahr now kept their eyes open. "Sight is complemented by sound. The green hue and moss sand and swirling beams of purple and Muscari light in the sky each grow in beauty when a wind leaps through the palms as tall as three, rustling branches. A dish of fresh fruits and ripe nuts captures the laughter of small ones nearby and glows with their joy of the day. The green and purple birds with bright orange feet of your gold sand splash in pools and speak in verse, perfecting the sky and sea to any listening ear. Even what you see—the green and purple feathers and their bright orange feet—depend upon the smells and tastes and sounds of the sea."

The boy thought back to the gold sand and those birds, flying and tapping and splashing.

"Sound alone is a gift," Albahr continued. "Close your eyes and lie, boy."

The boy lay on the white sand, breathing easy and eager for another song.

"Hear the near cascade. It capers from rock to mossed rock to felled palm before diving under and joining the current. It bubbles and splashes. Dance with the individual sounds you hear. Let them pass you from one to the next. Appreciate the lonesome notes of rock and felled palm and the current and bubbles and splashes, then the melody as it rises."

The boy heard the cascade and understood the caper and found lonesome notes climbing. He held dear the simple sounds of water running over rock or through mossed rock or around felled palm. Still, the melody rose. His mind was filled with water: frigid and capering and bubbling and splashing through the dry orchard of immense palms.

"Now fall with it. Let the song of the cascade pull you under and consume your place."

The boy fell with the melody and felt the whole song of the cascade run through him. He shivered, smelling and tasting and hearing and afraid to open his eyes for fear it might all go away. His mind danced over the water and the moss of the mossed rock touched his skin. He tasted grey and pink stone and he felt the current of the underwater pull him deeper into sensation. He saw the whole orchard of palms as tall as three and smooth, fine sand die and live again by this cascade and die and grow into what it now was. The boy saw all the roots and fruit and nut trees of the basin, and he smelled them in the water and tasted their black dirt in the air above it. His drowning eyes followed each drop of water; some fell on stone, others were drawn into sand, and still more fell into the easy basin, wetting the black dirt of its bank. He clung to the skin of small ones cooling from their chase and wet the bony feet of bathing birds. All lived of the cascade.

The boy thought of the forest and the sea and the reefs, and their songs tore desire from him. He thought of the blue rock mountains and the Punica and lemons growing on their sides and the sand beyond. Happy envy for any there now poured from his heart.

The boy opened his eyes. As he sat, he squinted at his dream friends. He inhaled to his stomach and exhaled to his head. Had it been real? Albahr and the white bird formed as the boy's eyes adjusted. Albahr smiled and the boy knew it real. His heart raced with affection for sensation and its participants.

"You know the medicine for war-harm," the white bird said.

"How can I know it if I know not war-harm?" the boy asked, his brow furrowing.

"You know war-harm," the white bird said. "You have seen it and you will see it again."

The boy thought hard and his eyes narrowed.

"War-harm threatens when any gathered together do not live in the Joy of Senses. It is not an enemy from here or far, as small ones and the Misled speculate, but is within anyone carrying captivation other than in the Joy of Senses," the white bird said.

"War-harm travels as a sea wind; all feel its force and all guess from where it came, and it moves without spectator and it fills the mouths of the guessers. It is the collective exhale of those who do not see the simple truths of the sea man."

"His smile moors us to the island and to each other and cannot be learned, only experienced," the boy said.

"The sea man smiled, boy, because of these truths. He saw the green and purple birds with bright orange feet of your sand and heard their splashes and verse. He saw more than birds, boy, and he heard more than splashes and verse."

"The Joy of Senses moors us to the island," the boy said.

"The sea man saw his wife and son in the green and purple birds with bright orange feet. He heard his wife's voice in their spoken poems and his son's laughter in their splashing. He knew his loss served beauty. His wife could sing with the green and purple birds with bright orange feet and his son could splash in sea pools with these. There they lived, even in death! Without the Joy of Senses, loss of the loved is pain. With the Joy of Senses, we are moored to the island and to each other; there is no loss, only the union of one's spirit to the island for the love of all," the white bird said.

Albahr ceded with a nod and stood. The white bird rested on his shoulder.

The boy stood and closed his eyes. He thought hard. He saw himself young, watching his mother prepare an orange fruit. She peeled the skin and rubbed it in her hands and smelled her hands. She breathed and closed her eyes and smiled. She tasted the orange fruit and closed her eyes and smiled again. Now she held a lime. The boy watched her peel the skin and rub the lime in her hands and smell her hands. She breathed and closed her eyes and smiled. She tasted the lime and closed her eyes and smiled again.

"He smiled for his loss because it was not loss at all," the boy said, eyes closed. "In the Joy of Senses there is no loss, only the songs of what is now and what has gone."

The boy's thoughts churned and still his eyes were closed.

He thought to return to the gold sand and tell his journey. He yearned for the sea and reefs, curious to fall into their songs. No, he thought, Dahlia must come to know the Joy of Senses. What might some journey home, and the journey told, be with no companion? Who to witness his time with the three frightful creatures and in the forest and among the people of the palms as tall as three? Dahlia felt far away as he stood near the cascade, eyes closed. It was dread and solitude, fear for his friend never knowing the sea man's smile. The boy opened his eyes.

Albahr and the white bird were gone.

Fifteen

AT SUNSET, when the sand turned to moss sand and the green hue filled the orchard, Dahlia sat with the boy and all the people of the palms as tall as three. The two sat in silence, the boy in the Joy of Senses and Dahlia in anticipation of their journey to the Men.

When the light in the sky turned from Muscari to emerald and all lay on the white sand to rest, the boy asked Dahlia to stay longer in the orchard that they might adventure together. He could not explain this adventure, and Dahlia was lost to the journey ahead. His friend would not be delayed and the boy worried. He replayed his words and Dahlia's words and wondered if he failed to convince his friend on staying. Dahlia was resolved to leave after two sunrises.

"Will others join the journey?" the boy asked.

"We will travel as two," Dahlia said. "Those I met will wait too long. They fear the forest."

"They have heard, then," the boy said, his mind on the three figures.

"Rest, friend."

Just before sunrise, when the orchard was still and dark, Dahlia told the boy the two would leave that sunrise, not the next. This urgency surprised the boy, and he wanted to stay and speak with Albahr and the white bird longer. He asked Dahlia to stay one more day; he enjoyed his time with the people of the palms as tall as three. Dahlia enjoyed it as much, but the white shimmer still danced in the forest and eluded the Men.

The boy sat by the river as Dahlia said goodbye to the taller and the freckled and their mother and father and gathered four orange fruits and a hand of ripe nuts for the journey. He thought of how he would tell Dahlia he was not going on the journey to the Men and that he wanted to stay with the people of the palms as tall as three before returning to the gold sand. He felt lost to gain Dahlia's trust from the Men. Such rush and little desire discouraged the boy. Did he hear the songs of the breeze and cascade well for his father's warning of the Men and the white shimmer? Could Dahlia ever know the Joy of Senses? The boy did not want his friend to stay in the forest with the Men; one might never see the other again. Tears welled in his eyes. He scooped white sand in his hands and put it to his nose and smiled, though he was still sad.

Dahlia bowed to those waving and looked at the boy with sand to his nose. The boy rose and walked to Dahlia, his abandonment of their journey drooping his shoulders and puffing his lip.

Dahlia was proud and happy and wrestled the orange fruits, near dropping one. The boy took two and prepared his words.

"Dahlia."

Dahlia grinned and looked to the expanse of sand and palms stretching away to the forest. "We might rest at the basin and enjoy something new. It was bad to leave there without even a handful of rubyroot."

The boy looked into the great orchard, too, away from the palm mats stretched about. His eyes found Dahlia's. I will save my friend from the white shimmer, he thought. Dahlia will not fall into the sneaking and hunting.

"Come, friend," Dahlia said. "I have four orange fruits and a hand of ripe nuts for our journey."

The boy's heart beat fast and he felt nervous in the still, hot air.

He swallowed hard and offered his friend a trusting smile. "And we will still rest at the basin?"

Dahlia laughed. "Yes."

The boy's eyes climbed an immense palm. He wished he could sit atop it and watch their journey unfold. He wished he could take Dahlia there and see the Men from the safety of the orchard. He wished Albahr and the white bird cared for Dahlia's attention.

The two walked toward the cascade and turned alongside it. The distant forest, out of sight past the palms as tall as three, loomed dark.

Sixteen

THE BOY AND DAHLIA spoke little as they walked. Past the ample basin, the two were again lost to the dry expanse of palms as tall as three. The boy's feet sank in the sand and his tongue dried in the still, hot air. He closed his eyes and inhaled with such gentleness he was afraid not to smell at all, remembering Albahr's words about being gentle. Dry rock and salt and young palm branches filled his nose. He let it pass to his ears and opened his mouth, and the boy tasted sand and lemons and palm bark.

The Joy of Senses needs patience, he thought. Walking about and mindful of this journey, it is hard to hear any song. I might sit quiet and still if not for this haste. Still, there is always some song; it must be attended even in distraction. To miss such adventure of sensation . . .The boy shook his head and closed his eyes again, still walking.

Even in the boredom of the immense orchard, away now from any ease of familiarity, day hurried to night. Musings and curiosities crept away in the black of the night and the two slept well.

THE NEXT DAY, wet moss and black, teeming dirt filled the boy's nose. He tasted rotting palms and flowering trees and knew the forest was near. He smiled, eager to fall into the song of the forest.

"The forest is near, Dahlia."

"I will be happy to walk on solid floor," Dahlia said. "Sunset is near too. Let's make the forest and walk again at sunrise."

"The forest is good to rest."

As the boy smelled, the forest came and the two said goodbye to the orchard of palms as tall as three and smooth, fine sand. The boy thought of Albahr and the white bird and his new Joy of Senses. Dahlia thought of the taller and the freckled and their mother and father and the pleasant basin and the stillness of the air.

On the edge of the forest and before sunset, the two found a rubyroot patch and rested there, the boy against a wide, mossed stump. They enjoyed rubyroot and sat in silence. Looking at Dahlia, the boy saw his friend was not surrounded by forest edge and did not stand on forest floor. Dahlia was with the Men, in pursuit of the white shimmer. Dahlia ran and climbed and laughed with the Men; the boy was not in this daydream. Dahlia sat in a circle with the Men and each took a bite from an orange fruit and passed it to the next. When it came, the boy watched his friend smell the fruit and smile. Dahlia tasted the fruit and smiled.

"Do you daydream?" Dahlia asked. The boy came back from his daydream to curious eyes. He blushed.

"Do you?" he asked.

"Often."

"What of?"

"My daydream is always the same: I stand before the white shimmer and it asks me—though it does not ask with words and I do not know how it asks—why I am standing before it. I always claim to be the special one. I reach out my hand, and the white shimmer is not there and I am alone in the forest."

The boy wondered if this caused Dahlia to doubt being the special one.

"What is your daydream?" Dahlia asked.

"This is a new one," the boy said.

"Is it a good story?"

"I do not know."

"Will you tell me?" Dahlia asked.

"I see you run and climb and laugh with the Men in pursuit of the white shimmer," the boy said.

Dahlia smiled. "You are with the Men and me?"

"I am not, though I see you run and climb and laugh. You and the Men sit in a circle and pass an orange fruit from one to the next. When it comes to you, you smell it and smile. You taste it and smile. That is the end," the boy said.

"Do you wonder if dreams and daydreams mean?" Dahlia asked.

"I am resolved they do," the boy said.

"What of these two daydreams?"

"May I speak as a friend?"

"You may speak as you are."

"Dahlia, I now would have told you these sooner. Many sunrises and sunsets ago, my wise father told me the sneaking and hunting is in vain. He said the white shimmer charms, it does not serve, and the Men are captivated by what they see and do not remember the truths of the sea man's smile. He told me the sea man is not in the white shimmer, but he is of the island and all things on the island."

Dahlia tasted a lime, and the boy watched his friend ponder these words.

"What of war-harm, if your wise father knows?" Dahlia asked. "The Men pursue the white shimmer to know the medicine for war-harm and to protect you and me and your father and mother and the people of the palms as tall as three and all."

"War-harm, Dahlia, does not threaten from the outside. War-harm is from within. It is where any gather and do not experience the Joy of Senses, which Albahr and the white bird gave me. We have seen war-harm in the three figures, and I believe we will see it again with the Men. This our daydreams mean."

Dahlia's cheeks turned red.

"The Joy of Senses is wonderful. My daydream of you smelling and tasting the orange fruit and smiling is you in the Joy of Senses. And yours is the charm of the white shimmer. It does not serve," the boy said.

"Tell me this Joy of Senses," Dahlia said.

"Smells and tastes ought to be enjoyed with appreciation for their character, whether good or bad. They are diverse. Enjoyment in these comes from closing your eyes and imagining the colors and life of the smell or taste. I find an individual piece in my mind and let it cause feeling. I pass on to the next."

"The life of the smell or taste?" Dahlia asked with a small smile.

"Yes."

"Are smells and tastes different?"

"Smells give gentle pictures. Grasses and blossoms and ripe nuts are my favorites. Streams, too. I close my eyes and they drift through me, painting as only grasses and blossoms and ripe nuts and streams are able. Tastes have spirit—they are vivid, even the smallest seed. These limes and ripe nuts, each its own, charm my heart to forest adventure. Rubyroot buries my legs in the forest floor, like small trunks. I feel like I've lived forever in dirt and sweet sugar leaves."

"You have thought much."

"Only as much as time I have. If I am not smelling or tasting, I can see. If my eyes are closed, I dance with sound. When I lie in quiet, the air or wind or floor are still present.

"Of sight and sound, Albahr and the white bird taught me this: sight is complemented by sound. Look at the floor," the boy said.

"I see brown and green, I see palm bark and roots, I see a night bird's print and hard stones," Dahlia said.

"Now hear the cool stream." The boy pointed to the sound of moving water past the forest's edge. "Hear the stream and let it move through the brown and green, the palm bark and roots, over the night bird's print and hard stones. The stream, trickling nearby, gives life to the forest floor. The floor lays home for brown and green, for palm bark and roots, for the night bird's print and hard stones. Imagine the stream, trickling nearby, rising and falling and rising again. It washes away the night bird's print and makes way for a forest deer. It carries palm bark and hard stones on. A blossom plant roots. The brown and green become sky blue and mantis orange and emerald and Punica red. See the brown and green and hear what they will become."

Dahlia stood tranced at the boy's words. A dull forest floor lay. When the stream trickled nearby, however, the dull forest floor had life and intention. It turned vivid and morphed into a blossoming garden as the stream rose and fell and rose and covered it and moved through it.

Dahlia looked at the boy and back at the floor.

"Smell that felled palm," the boy said.

"It looks rot."

"Tell me what you smell. Smell with such gentleness you might not smell at all."

Moved by visions of the forest floor, Dahlia bent and studied the felled palm. Creatures fiddled. Mossed and trodden, the log was ordinary and unworthy of a passer's time.

"Smell with such gentleness," the boy reminded.

First, wet moss and burrowing creatures. With eyes closed, Dahlia smelled ripe nuts and strong wood and fresh palm. Smelling with such gentleness, the rot wood took on colors of smell and shades of colors of smell. Dahlia smelled rain and wind as taking to a cave during a storm would arouse. The life of the palm, felled and rot, lived in smell. Dahlia saw the sapling, saw it grow tall into a strong palm, and saw it return to the floor in this heap of rot.

Dahlia's face changed from smelling a felled palm to smelling the life of a felled palm. The boy smiled and laughed. He told Dahlia to let the smell pass to the ears and fill the mouth and let the felled palm whisper in the mouth. "It touches the tongue, now the roof and the cheeks, and now you feel it on your throat."

Dahlia smiled too, with eyes closed, and let a laugh escape.

That first night back in the forest, the boy danced with cricket chirps and howling creatures. He was passed between trickling streams and rustling ferns and night birds' loos. He appreciated each of these. In his mind he saw vines climbing and trees growing and stones wearing smooth by stream; it was the melody of the night forest. He fell with it. He allowed the song of the night forest to envelop him, consuming his place. The boy sat there, his back resting on a wide, mossed stump, and smiled at the new and beautiful.

Seventeen

"I WILL STILL GO to the Men," Dahlia said as the two enjoyed a sunrise rubyroot. "The Joy of Senses is wonderful, as you said, but it does not mean the sneaking and hunting is in vain. It may be more wonderful in the white shimmer, friend. Why can we not show the Men your Joy of Senses? Though it would surprise me if these did not know it already."

Dahlia's eyes were for the Men and the white shimmer. The boy thought to leave Dahlia and return to the people of the palms as tall as three, or to return to the gold sand and be with his father and mother. Sadness washed over him; he had to wipe his eye. He blushed and was glad Dahlia did not see.

"I will come with you to the Men, Dahlia," the boy said. "You are my friend and your adventure is mine. I hope the Men know the Joy of Senses and I hope the white shimmer is the spirit of the sea man."

Dahlia smiled.

The boy resolved to encourage Dahlia in the Joy of Senses. He saw Dahlia's eyes were for the Men, but thought to change that with time. He wondered if Dahlia would realize the charm of the white shimmer. He smiled and thought, not proud but determined.

The two walked and the boy encouraged.

"Dahlia," the boy would say, "do you smell that blossom?"

Or "My friend, can you taste that young palm in the air?"

Later, the boy would ask, "Do you taste this breeze?"

As the sun climbed above the palms of the forest, the two thought to find a place to rest. The boy was tired from the night song, and he thought Dahlia tired from his encouragement. The two had walked in the forest edge as the father of the taller and the freckled instructed, crossing two streams. Now they looked for another.

They found another. Rubyroot and blossoms and cobnut trees and lime trees grew at this stream. The two enjoyed many tastes, and the boy enjoyed many smells and sounds.

"This is a good place to rest," he said.

"Yes," Dahlia said.

The two rested on boulders separated by a rubyroot patch. Dahlia slept first.

When the boy awoke, the sun was still high above the palms of the forest and Dahlia was gone, though the boy was not alone.

He was surrounded by grey forest deer.

The closest had brown spots on the legs. Another, white spots. The grey fur appeared brushed smooth; it shined in the sun. The boy thought them ancient and special. He hoped Dahlia's return would not startle the quiet assembly. Quite large, the smallest stood tall in the deepest bend of the stream.

The forest deer, grey and large and quiet, had eyes as dark and green as night forest. Some had a small set of horns that, white as clouds, rose straight and curled into tight spirals. Some ate grasses, some nuzzled the dirt for rubyroot, and others cooled in the stream.

The boy thought the forest deer would smell of fur or old grass—it was what he imagined—but the elegant creatures perfumed the air with yellow apple, rubyroot, lemon, and palm bark. When one moved by, the boy smelled cobnut and moss.

He slid from his boulder and stood among the grey and large and quiet.

Dahlia appeared, clutching a heap of round, orange fruits.

The boy watched Dahlia lower the fruits and smile. His companion looked to laugh without sound.

These two meandered through the forest deer, taking care to practice quiet and not disturb the creatures. Dahlia was intrigued by the smell, the boy lost in what his eyes saw.

As the boy or Dahlia passed a forest deer, the dark eyes would follow. Soon, the head would lower and the grazing or nuzzling would resume. Some became inquisitive and followed Dahlia or the boy, perhaps engaged in their own Joy of Senses at the two-legged.

The boy, once comfortable in his movement, put his hands on the side of one. He closed his eyes and understood, beyond sight and smell and sound and taste, the forest deer. He felt the heart jump and lungs fill and empty; he felt the muscle and skin and fur and understood the forest deer as he understood himself. It wasn't grey fur to marvel or a perfume of yellow apple, rubyroot, lemon, and palm bark to smell; this grey forest deer was alive! It breathed and moved and created beauty in the forest. Without this creature, this creature of grey with white and brown spots, the forest would not exist as it is. The wind would not smell so and the cool stream would not taste so and the rubyroot would not be so enjoyable. The sun, wind, stream, leaves, rocks, palms and all the forest would not exist in song as they do.

The boy opened his eyes. The forest deer looked at him. He saw himself in the eyes of the creature.

Without spectator, a white bird landed on the boulder where the boy had rested. Without spectator, it flew away.

Eighteen

THE BOY KNEW he and Dahlia neared the Men when the air tasted and the floor looked like it had in his dream the first night he and Dahlia spent together in the forest. The dust was thinner and the forest held green and the air did not smell so rot, but still the boy knew because he had never seen the dust or tasted this taste except in his dream.

The pair, still walking in the forest edge, reached a path of felled palms which coursed away from the orchard of palms as tall as three and smooth, fine sand. The boy saw vines climbing across it and blossoms shooting through the felled palms. Mosses crept along the edge. He was surprised to see rubyroot and a patch of small palms making new growth. He thought the path had not been walked in many sunrises and sunsets.

This felled-palm path coursed deep into the forest until the still, hot air of the orchard was forgotten and the smooth, fine sand which the boy's feet sank into could have only been a dream.

When the sun dropped from its perch high above the canopy, the felled-palm path opened to another. It was a long and wide clearing that stretched in front of the boy and Dahlia and ran until they could not see it in either direction. The floor of it was stomped by many feet and it too was lined with felled palm trunks. Voices of excitement carried from one direction. From the other came evening sounds of the forest.

"What will we say? They do welcome new often?" Dahlia wondered aloud as the two turned to face the voices.

"I do not know," the boy said.

There the pair stood with fear and excitement and curiosity and the song of the forest behind them.

Dahlia took the first step. The boy took his and the evening sounds of the forest disappeared under laughs and yelps of entertainment.

"They do not seem to sneak and hunt now," the boy said.

Dahlia looked to the sky. "Sunset is near. They must near sunrise."

The boy felt the late warmth of the day along this trodden felled-palm path. I hope to find a new song here, the song of the Men, and have it join the song of the cascade and the song of the forest in the Joy of Senses, he thought. He hoped Dahlia would not forget the Joy of Senses during their time with the Men. How long will we stay among them? Dahlia thinks we will learn of the sneaking and hunting, and my friend or I may be the special one or we will wait for the special one. For how long? Is my wise father right that the sneaking and hunting is in vain and the white shimmer does not serve? I wish to know the sea man. I want to see the blue rocks mountains and again the orchard of palms as tall as three and smooth, fine sand and hear their songs. Will I see Albahr and the white bird again?

Round a bend of this felled-palm path, the boy and Dahlia saw the Men for the first time. The sun lowered, and the forest held green darkness throughout. The Men were in a clearing and danced around some great fire, one with a spiraled black cloud pouring from its top. They laughed and danced and dunked their heads in a tall water bath to keep cool. This great fire burned loud, and they dunked their heads. The boy smelled the fire and tasted the dust and the black cloud and felt the air hot. It was not like the warmth of sun; it fell on the face and skin and not the nose and lips, and it did not warm from the inside or make the boy shiver. The heat only made the boy wish for a cool stream and the song of the forest or the song of the cascade. The Men were captive of this fire.

Each of the dancing Men stopped and a shell, one like the boy would see in a sea pool near their sturdy wood home, was passed between them. Others sat outside the circle of dance and laughs, The Men, captivated by the great fire, each put the blue and orange and smooth and long shell to their mouths and tasted with reverence. Words were said by one and the others repeated.

"Did you hear that?" Dahlia asked the boy.

"No," the boy said.

"They mentioned the white shimmer."

The boy and Dahlia stood without spectator where the felled-palm path met the clearing of the Great Fire.

"I would think to wait until this is done," the boy said as Dahlia stepped forward.

"Yes," his friend replied. Both sat and waited.

Soon the organized dance and laughter ended, and the Men sat amongst themselves, conversing. It was an inviting scene against the Great Fire, and one approached the boy and Dahlia. "Have you come to see the Men?"

"Yes," Dahlia said.

The man swung his arm back.

"I see you all," Dahlia said.

"You see us. And have you come here to join the Men?" he asked.

"We have come to learn of the sneaking and hunting." Dahlia and the one who approached held their eyes. They spoke without words. Dust fell heavy and rested on shoulders and heads and hands and feet. The spiraled black cloud shifted once or twice but held its course.

"Many have come to see the Men and a few to join the Men in the sneaking and hunting. You"—this one looked at each—"come to join the Men in sneaking and hunting."

"We come to learn," Dahlia said. The boy had no words.

"Once you learn, you join. Not on our account, but the sea man's," this one said.

Dahlia and the boy looked at each other. The boy nodded and Dahlia took this one's hand in one hand and the boy's hand in the other. The three, linked by hand, walked along the edge of the clearing to the opposite side and went again into the green darkness held by the forest. They left behind the heavy dust fall and the heat of the Great Fire and the tall water bath and the blue and orange and smooth and long shell and the captive. They left behind their fear and the song of the forest and the song of the cascade. The boy and Dahlia left behind the Joy of Senses.

Nineteen

THE BOY, fear left behind, wondered how many lived here. He wondered where they would go now. He wondered what would come of him and his companion amongst the Men. He wished he could speak to Dahlia without words.

With only a few steps, the three left the green even-more-darkness held by the forest and came to a grass field.

The one turned and spoke: "Here we grow rubyroot and yuca and ginger and arrowroot." The man's arm not holding Dahlia swung out and around. The patch was large and a large heap of ginger and yuca lay to one side.

Behind the far side of the patch, forest homes stood anchored by palms which grew through the center of each. "Here we live. Rest awhile."

The boy and Dahlia sat to rest. Their guide disappeared among the homes. "Let's eat the rest of our rubyroot," the boy said.

"Fine." The two sat and Dahlia said, "You did not speak about your brother."

"I have not seen my brother for many sunrises and sunsets. I will wait."

"Pass a rubyroot."

"They are ripe."

"Yes."

A patient curiosity like the kind the boy knew from watching his mother and sitting with his father for many sunrises and sunsets when he was small settled between the two. There were no words or laughs or stories and musings. The boy and Dahlia each resigned to their own thoughts and wondered, with no rush of time, what this place meant. The boy rested his palms on the floor. He closed his eyes and the Great Fire burned loud. He smelled and tasted dust. There was no song in the Joy of Senses for the boy to fall into. He wondered if Dahlia noticed.

The man returned and brought Dahlia and the boy to a home, creaky and comfortable in the nighttime, dusty forest. It had a sitting place and two palm beds for sleeping. "Rest here until sunrise. After sunrise, you will meet more and see more and learn."

The forest, darkening outside, was quiet. Forest birds and creatures felt far away.

"How are you?" Dahlia asked, noticing the boy's disturbance at the place.

"The Joy of Senses is quiet here," the boy said.

"I had not noticed."

"Have you now?"

"Have I now?"

"Noticed?"

"No."

The boy thought not Dahlia as cold or quiet, only that his friend had not experienced the Joy of Senses as he had. He wanted to explore more with his friend, but Dahlia's mind was on the Men and the white shimmer. His was on their lack of song.

AT SUNRISE, the one who first approached opened the door of their forest home and welcomed them again. His voice—much changed from the night before—was quick and bounced about the forest as he described the lay of their home. The boy and Dahlia had walked the preferred avenue of entrance and exit from their home, that felled-palm path. The thick and dense forest surrounding their home slows; the path permits speed and efficiency, he said. He explained how the Men cleared a path through the forest from their home and to a not-so-distant lake where the Men gathered water. They felled the palms, he said, by burning through the trunks with fire of the Great Fire.

The boy frowned.

Their path of felled palms led to the Great Fire, the clearing where the boy and Dahlia met this one. This clearing allowed the Men to give the Great Fire home. Dahlia asked why it needed a home. The guide said the Great Fire would empty of heat and flame if left unattended; it was best to keep it in one place for attendance. The boy asked why the Men needed the Great Fire. He learned the Great Fire gave the Men life and fellowship. The boy asked what fellowship meant. The man told the boy and Dahlia fellowship is a purposed community.

"Without the Great Fire, where would we dance and sing and prepare meal?" he asked.

The boy and Dahlia saw the Men tended the rubyroot and yuca and ginger and arrowroot in the grass field and tended lime and cobnut and lemon trees in a field near the not-so-distant lake. The forest homes gave the Men rest. (And did the two like their forest home? They did). Some were built many sunrises and sunsets ago and others smelled of fresh palm. The three wandered and spoke on fruits and ripe nuts and roots and the forest homes and the Great Fire burning loud and the felled-palm path and the not-so-distant lake.

The guide asked Dahlia and the boy from where they came and why they came and what they hoped. The boy and Dahlia were modest. Had they known each other long? They had not. Why did the boy come here? To learn of the sea man. The guide was excited by this. Dahlia came to catch the white shimmer. A good hunter, the man noted.

At the not-so-distant lake, the three sat for a bowl of mix. Dried lemon and lime and rubyroot and cobnut powder delighted the boy and Dahlia.

"The sun is high," the man said. "We rest when the sun is high."

"When do you sneak and hunt?" the boy asked.

"We pursue the white shimmer when it shows. It does not always show."

"It hides?" Dahlia asked.

"Yes. It has hidden now for three sunrises and two sunsets. We will see it soon. This is why others call it sneaking: we do not always see the white shimmer and we must sneak."

"The white shimmer will show soon?" Dahlia asked with a smile.

"Yes. It is real. You will see. We always have Men in the woods sneaking. They will find it and come say so."

"What now?" the boy asked.

"We rest, we fellowship, and we wait." The man looked to the sun and smiled. The boy wondered if the man was expressing thanks for the warmth.

The boy felt comfortable with their guide. "My brother is said to come here. Do you know him?"

"We renounce our old," the guide said. "Your brother may be here, or he may have left. He would not say if he saw you and would deny if you saw him."

"Some leave?" Dahlia asked.

The boy felt sad. Surely his brother would greet him. Surely he would greet his brother.

"Some leave. The white shimmer demands. The pursuit is hard and some will not wait when it does not show or when our hunting fails." The guide smiled and said, "Our pursuit is the toil of the sea man. He walked on the sea and endured many hard times for it, and now we pursue and endure many hard times for it."

Dahlia gave the boy a knowing and hopeful and excited glance. The boy felt excitement too.

"Near sunset, you will watch fellowship and the dance and laughs. You will meet others."

As the three sat under the high sun eating fresh fruits and ripe nuts and rubyroot, and the man gave the two sweet yuca, the boy marveled the lake. It was a deep blue and from where they sat resting, the boy could see turtles docked on a floating log. Unlike the sea of his home, the lake was as flat as a wide river stone. It did not move or thrash or spill onto the moss where the three sat. It lived to serve the turtles and the fish and the Men. The grey forest deer too. One turtle slipped from the log into the river stone lake and small waves broke. These ripples spread until the whole of the flat lake teemed with ripples. Still, it flattened back. Again, it was like the water had never been touched.

"By the sea," the boy said, "there are green and purple birds with bright orange feet. In the evening, these fly into the forest to rest. Have you seen them?"

"No," the guide said. "If I had, I would know. I have seen many forest birds and night forest birds with their cries and loos, but never a green and purple bird with bright orange feet."

The boy returned to the flat lake. He looked to the sky and noticed dust from the Great Fire moving with any breeze. He touched the moss where they sat. He closed his eyes and listened to the flat lake. He tasted the air and smelled. The song of the lake was quiet, if it even existed. This, and the mystery of his brother, saddened the boy. He wanted to fall into a song. None sang.

The guide recommended resting in the sun for a time and the three closed their eyes and slept.

Twenty

THE MAN WOKE FIRST and looked at the boy and Dahlia sleeping.

The boy was curious enough. He thought much of the forest and the forest floor and the lake and the grass field and plants and even rocks and roots. He was intrigued and troubled by the dust of the Great Fire. He often sat with his palms flat on the ground. He often closed his eyes. He often wanted to taste things. He is a strange boy, the man thought. He will make for a good thinker and sneaker.

Dahlia, the man thought, is focused. The white shimmer holds this one's attention. He wondered if Dahlia thought to be the special one, the one who would approach the white shimmer. Most did when they came. Maybe there is a special one out there. He shook his head. The sneaking and hunting, the pursuit, was hard because it was the toil of the sea man. They should not be allowed to approach without reverence. It requires great effort; there is much to gain. War-harm must be prevented.

He looked again at the sleeping two. Then the flat lake. He put his palms flat on the ground. He closed his eyes. He tasted a piece of moss. The man shrugged and let out his breath.

I wonder how these two will take to dunking in the tall ferment bath and eating the grey forest deer, the man thought. The executions, too.

Twenty-One

THE BOY WOKE on the moss near the not-so-distant lake with heavy thoughts. He dreamed again of the lake of fire and the turtles and where he sat now, upon waking, was where he sat in the dream. The boy had no time to think on this; Dahlia woke and the three spoke. The speaking felt aimless and kept his mind from exploring his dreams and the boy tapped his fingers on his leg.

Two others came from the felled-palm path and greeted the three speaking. Excitement shone on their faces, and the man who rested with the boy and Dahlia pressed them for their excitement.

"The sea man has returned, friends. Past the far side of our path." The other who spoke swung his arm in the direction of the forest.

The Men wanted the boy and Dahlia to see the white shimmer before the pursuit.

"It does not flee until pursued? It does not move?" Dahlia asked, rising from the moss.

The guide, the one who first greeted the boy and Dahlia, smiled.

"It remains where found until we give pursuit," one replied.

An eager thrill lifted the boy from dreams and turtles and sensation. "May we see it?"

"Yes. Come."

The three followed the two others back to the felled-palm path, away from the not-so-distant lake, and walked toward the home of the Men. Sneakers and hunters and others moved about with haste. The felled-palm path became like the cascade of the orchard of palms as tall as three and smooth, fine sand. Men capered and dove and bubbled and splashed with the current of others and others with theirs.

"It remains until approached. Do not approach it," one said to another, passing the boy and Dahlia's group.

"I have yet to see it at all; I helped to build forest homes when the white shimmer last came," another said.

"Maybe the special one is here," one said to two others.

The group of five gathered near where the white shimmer was said to be. Still, the cascade of others. Again, the boy and Dahlia were told to only observe; they nodded and agreed not to approach the white shimmer.

Each stepped into the forest from the felled-palm path, one after the other. Thick and green lush clung and wrapped and obstructed. The leader of the five trampled and clawed and uprooted, tearing a path for any to come after.

The air was thick with water from the sun and the not-so-distant lake and it reminded the boy of sea spray, but he did not taste salt. He missed the sea and the reefs and the green and purple birds with bright orange feet. The boy noticed the forest here was free of dust; the canopy overhead was dense and caught it falling. He closed his eyes and let the forest sea spray come into him. His hope for a rising melody and after, a song, left, and he was with the Men and Dahlia.

The lush opened and eased and they came to a rock formation. It was brown rock, smooth and tall, and the shape was steep. This formation was as high as the tallest of the five and the group gathered near it.

"Walk to the opposite side of this rock"—the man pointed to the top and over the formation—"and we will stand with our backs and hands near touching it." He raised his finger and eyebrows to the boy and Dahlia to make sure each understood. The boy and Dahlia nodded.

The two others in front, the guide third from the front, and Dahlia and the boy made way around the brown rock formation, smooth and tall. Soon, they reached the other side. The group lined with their backs near touching the formation.

There, in the sight of the five, stood the white shimmer.

Twenty-Two

DAHLIA WOKE on the moss near the not-so-distant lake with excitement to learn more from the guide. This excitement did not last; he was busy to keep them occupied and away from activity. Dahlia hid frustration for acceptance.

When the two Men arrived and spoke of the white shimmer, the excitement returned. At last Dahlia would come face-to-face with the sea man, the one pursued by many.

Could I be the special one? Dahlia wondered as the five walked the felled-palm path.

Dahlia thought to ignore the man's warning about approaching the white shimmer. They may forgive one new as excitable and eager to join the sneaking and hunting. The Men might be glad for such excitement and eagerness.

The brown rock formation reminded Dahlia of a stone home. It was in the shape of a home with other small homes jutting off and had windows and crevices and a sitting place and was quite pretty with moss and vines hanging from its flat top. As the five made way around, Dahlia again considered approaching the white shimmer. Am I the special one? Dahlia thought so.

Careful not to fall on a rock or a root or a tangled vine, Dahlia navigated with the eyes and did not raise them until each back and hand was near touching the formation and all the other eyes raised.

There, in the sight of Dahlia and the others, stood the white shimmer.

Eyes falling on the white shimmer, the forest vibrated with purpose. Dahlia touched each finger to the rock formation to steady the senses, but it was in vain. An aroma of nectar and Punica and lime and moss and cool stream and flat lake and forest floor floated in translucent drops of color. Each drop hung in Dahlia's bright eyes. The air moved in waves and Dahlia could see the breath of each of the five. Trees swayed and rocks throbbed and roots grew where they rested. Vines tangled and untangled. The green of the day forest intensified and turned to new greens and shades of blue and white. Dahlia took the fingers from the brown rock formation and looked at the hands. Each vein flowed with the energy of the white shimmer and its energy erupted from the fingertips, dissipating in a pretty blood-red stream of fine thread. Dahlia looked through all this to the white shimmer resting in stark contrast to the forest and laughed out loud. I should approach, Dahlia thought.

One step forward. And another. Then arms restraining. Leaves of the ground turned to dust and regrew where they had rested as new trees, and these trees swayed and danced with the ripples of air coming from the white shimmer.

Dahlia turned to the boy. "The song of the white shimmer is like no other song I have danced."

He did not respond. Dahlia watched the boy's eyes move from the forest to the group and back to the forest where the white shimmer stood.

Still the forest vibrated with purpose.

Dahlia, eyes closed, listened to birds' wings and creatures' steps. Each sound came at Dahlia like a thread, and all threads wove into the song of the white shimmer. A palm rustled and joined. A drop of water fell nearby and joined. The breathing of the five joined.

Louder the forest vibrated with purpose.

Dahlia's eyes opened and fell again on the white shimmer.

Twenty-Three

THE BOY did not respond to Dahlia. His friend was deep into what the white shimmer was saying. He heard it too.

The boy heard and saw and felt and tasted and smelled all Dahlia heard and saw and felt and tasted and smelled. It was nectar and Punica and lime and moss and cool stream and flat lake and forest floor floating in translucent drops of color. The boy saw the air move in waves and the breath of the five. Trees swayed and rocks throbbed and roots grew where they rested. Vines tangled and untangled. The green of the day forest intensified and turned to new greens and shades of blue and white. Each vein in the boy's hands flowed with the energy of the white shimmer and its energy erupted from his fingertips, dissipating in a pretty blood-red—and a bit of purple!—stream of fine thread.

The boy, though aware of all, did not want to approach. He saw Dahlia take one step forward. And another. He knew his friend should not and he restrained.

Dahlia turned to the boy. "The song of the white shimmer is like no other song I have danced."

The boy felt the song of the white shimmer too. Another, though, danced in it. Someone else, not any of the five or the white shimmer itself, danced in the forest with the song of the white shimmer.

It was a creature of emptiness, some ghoul with paranoid eyes and a hollow chest. When Dahlia stepped forward, it reached anxious arms out, eager for some partner in its wicked song. Another step and it leaned from the white shimmer, its eternal prison, calling to Dahlia.

Why do the Men and Dahlia not feel this emptiness? the boy wondered. In the reflections of their eyes, he saw the white shimmer's captives.

It was like the drops of nectar and Punica and lime and moss and cool stream and flat lake and forest floor floated in the air but did not take hold of his senses. There was a weakness to it. It was a vile whisper after a fresh sea wind. The perfume danced in the air and touched his nose and tongue and swirled around the five and captivated four of them. It rested on his tongue and nose and dispersed like a flock of green and purple birds with bright orange feet under threat of sea swell. It was gone. The perfume was not like a rot log or cool stream or the sun; it played and left. It did not fill, and he did not feel warmth or coolness, or the life of the forest grow and die and grow inside himself, though he watched it. Vines tangled and untangled, and the color of the day forest intensified. He saw the leaves of the ground turn to dust and sprout again where they rested as new trees and sway and dance with the waves of air coming from the white shimmer, but these new trees were gnarled and covered in the dust that now littered the once leaf-covered floor. These trees are not new life, the boy thought. These trees are born of the dust of the Great Fire.

The boy did not answer his companion. He looked at the white shimmer and back to the four and back to the white shimmer. Are you the sea man? the boy thought. He felt the empty creature within the fantastic display. He closed his eyes as Dahlia's opened and he heard birds' wings and creatures' steps and palms rustle and water drip and the breathing of the five.

Still, the boy longed. He longed for the white shimmer to hide, to experience what he saw without the empty ghoul watching. He felt as he were looking into a sea pool teeming with creatures and color and he longed to join them in song and dance beneath the surface. He saw and thought wonderful, but his senses could not participate for that empty creature, its paranoid eyes feasting on the four captivated.

The sea man was not in the white shimmer. Where then? He did not know. But time in the Joy of Senses kept him from falling under captivation by the white shimmer. Had Dahlia not known the Joy of Senses? He remembered his friend stopped more often to smell and taste and he remembered Dahlia's fascination with the rot log. Whether his demonstrations were inadequate or his friend had never taken an interest in the Joy of Senses, he did not know. Dahlia kept focus on the white shimmer, even before the two had reached the Men or come to this rock formation. Dahlia sought the white shimmer and the boy sought the sea man. Dahlia had been armed with stories and the boy had been armed with the Joy of Senses.

The white shimmer, his wise father taught, entertained and did not serve. Was this the entertainment, the captivation of the Men? The Men intend goodness, the boy remembered, but contribute not. Here they stood, four captivated and entertained to joy and purpose and one empty and in knowledge of the truth.

Have I already met the sea man? the boy wondered. Have I in the sand of the beach and the trees of the forest and the rocks and sea moss and fruits and ripe nuts and green and purple birds with bright orange feet and small claws and cool stream and grey forest deer and palms as tall as three and the freckled and the taller and the basin and the cascade? The boy did not know. He knew, however, the Joy of Senses, connecting him to each of these, was muted by the Great Fire and its dust and the white shimmer, entertaining the Men in the forest.

He did not want Dahlia to become like the captivated. What could he do? His friend saw all before the five and was charmed. Will I tell my companion of the empty creature lurking in the song?

He closed his eyes and opened them again, looking into the moving forest.

Is it real? he wondered. Are we five imagining this? If it is never to be caught and it does not serve, can it be real? His mind played in wondering if the white shimmer, standing and entertaining in the forest, soon to dance for the Men's pursuit, existed only in their minds and expectations. He closed and opened his eyes and closed them again, waiting for the white shimmer and its display to be gone, but it stayed. And stayed the boy, looking at this sea pool teeming with creatures and color, unable to participate in the song and dance beneath the surface.

The first of the five broke from their group and came around and led Dahlia and the boy by hand back to the other side. The other two Men followed. The guide observed them and asked what the two thought of the white shimmer.

The boy lowered his head and shifted his feet and thought for a response. Dahlia, though, leapt at the opportunity to discuss the white shimmer.

"It was like no other song I have danced," Dahlia said. "The white shimmer, the sea man, is beauty and life. The life and death of trees were on display and the vines and the air and the color—"

"The white shimmer is beauty," the man said. Dahlia's face was bright red and beaming with excitement and the man felt the wandering of speech. The boy looked over the man's shoulder now and whispered. "What did you say, boy?"

"The white shimmer is beauty," the boy lied. "The display was enchanting. May we return and see it again? I fear I may miss its display."

Dahlia smiled at him, and the boy saw his friend's eyes loose and heavy, as a tired person trying to return to some enchanted dream.

The man was satisfied by the boy's answer and clapped his hands in excitement at the boy's and Dahlia's enjoyment of and fascination in the white shimmer. The boy exhaled relief. Dahlia hugged him and thanked him. Though he knew not his worthiness of thanks, he accepted. The boy was now faced with a dilemma he may have avoided, he realized, had he listened to his wise father's words and his recent dreams.

Do the men seek the medicine for war-harm? he wondered. Do they seek the sea man and his wisdom or is the self at the head of their sneaking and hunting? They must wonder who will capture the sea man. Dahlia thinks to be the special one. There is no special one! My friend is Misled. Our guide said some leave, those who grow tired of waiting for the white shimmer to show, so I will leave. I will leave before this sunset. I will thank the Men and tell them I must return to the forest now. I hope Dahlia will come.

"We will go back to our forest homes now and prepare for sunset. We sneak and hunt with sunrise."

The boy and Dahlia and the guide returned by the felled-palm path to the Great Fire, which was attended by one, and through the clearing of the Great Fire to the grass field where the Men grew rubyroot, yuca, ginger, and arrowroot and through here to the forest homes.

"Wash yourselves there"—the man pointed through a row of trees—"in the stream. Drink, too. Rest and I will come for you. Do not leave until I come."

The boy and Dahlia washed their faces and enjoyed the stream.

It was less cool than their cool stream in the forest, the boy thought. He wondered if his view of this stream was wronged by his view of the Men. He hoped not. He tasted the water again.

"My friend," Dahlia said. "I am excited to pursue the white shimmer. I am excited to sneak and hunt and stay here and learn from the Men. Thank you for your company and for coming here. We have found the sea man!"

"Dahlia." The boy smiled like a mother watching a small one dance. "I am glad for your excitement of the white shimmer and the sneaking and hunting and staying here to learn from the Men. Your company is more than mine; this I know. For bringing me here, only you can I thank. I pursued the sea man when I came into the forest and you taught of your adventures and the Men. Now we have arrived here."

Dahlia smiled back at the boy.

He continued: "But before this sunset, I am leaving my friend and the Men and the white shimmer and the Great Fire and the not-so-distant lake and all else. I will miss you more than these. I will miss the grass field with rubyroot and yuca and ginger and arrowroot. I know I must leave, though now I do not know where I will go. Perhaps the blue rock mountains and the orchard of palms as tall as three and smooth, fine sand. I may return home; you saw from where I came into the forest."

Dahlia remained silent as he spoke, and when the boy finished, his companion's eyes fell to the forest floor.

"I do not wish your leaving," Dahlia said.

The boy wished not to offend his friend. "The Joy of Senses calls me. I have had dreams," he said.

"Dreams brought most here, and one's dreams take him back?" Dahlia asked.

"I cannot speak for most," the boy said.

"You do not believe the sea man is in the white shimmer."

The boy sighed and shrugged his shoulders. "How can I?"

"I can," Dahlia said with offense.

"I saw all you saw and all the other three saw. But there danced an empty creature in the song of the white shimmer. I cannot explain that. I dreamt of fire and dust and the white shimmer, and I do not believe the sea man is in the white shimmer. My wise father said the sea man is of the island. Albahr and the white bird which spoke man—you heard him— told me the white shimmer charms and does not serve. Could he be of the island and in the white shimmer? I suppose. Can he charm and hold the medicine for war-harm? I do not think so. The empty creature I saw melted my heart for this place."

Dahlia looked frustrated at his words. "You saw an empty creature and many others saw beauty."

"Some have left," the boy said.

"With not wanting to wait."

"He says."

"You do not trust our guide, the one who first greeted us and showed us fellowship?" Dahlia asked.

"I do not know our guide. I know my wise father and Albahr and the white bird," the boy said.

"Do you know me?"

"Dahlia, you are my friend and companion. With love I know you."

"Stay and see the sea man. Stay until the white shimmer is caught."

"I will leave before sunset."

Dahlia's frustration swelled and the two sat near the stream and drank and washed. They returned to the forest home and rested for a time. The boy's mind danced with guilt of friend and worry of destination and fear of speaking truth. When would he tell the guide he would leave? He supposed after the gathering for which they had washed and drank and now rested. He longed to return to the forest from this crowded and captive place. His impatience for the Joy of Senses grew.

He decided the first place to go was the orchard of the palms as tall as three and smooth, fine sand. He longed to tell Albahr and the white bird about the Men. He might stay awhile and wander and sleep under emerald light and eat Punica and lemons at the base of the blue rock mountains.

The boy smiled.

Next, he thought, I might venture into the blue rock mountains. Those mountains looked to the sky to learn of beauty and grew into their own. Their beauty was like the green and purple birds with bright orange feet or the grey forest deer or the taste of rubyroot or the smell of the sun. The boy wondered about the song of the blue rock mountains and shuddered as if their cold air, which he had never felt, filled his mouth and nose and ears.

The boy held his joy at his impending adventure. Dahlia had not spoken since returning to the forest home. To laugh now would offend more than he had already, he was sure.

After a time, the guide opened the door and invited the two outside and to the Great Fire for the gathering, the one that would mark the sneaking and hunting. Dahlia grew excited but spoke little to the boy. He was saddened at losing Dahlia and excited for his leaving. Curious about this gathering, he resolved to stay for it.

Their guide gathered ginger from a heap at their passing of the grass field and mentioned a meal. The boy looked forward to fresh fruits and ripe nuts and roots. Rested and clean and quenched by the stream and with a meal before leaving, he felt as though he were a fresh and soft sea foam under the warmth of the sun. He smiled.

Twenty-Four

THE THREE JOINED a group and crossed from the grass field to the Great Fire. It burned loud. Men filled the tall water bath. Strange perfumes lingered and swirled with the dust. The black cloud spiraled high.

Two spoke loud of the sneaking and hunting. Energy and laughter erupted between them and one touched the other's shoulder and the other touched his as they spoke and they both laughed. The boy thought their words strange in texture and their posture awkward.

Still, strange perfumes swirled with the dust.

All gathered in front of the Great Fire, like they were in the boy's dream, though none prostrated. Each sat. The boy and Dahlia and the guide were near the back, farthest from the heat.

Dahlia's eyes were wide. The boy's, unenthused but curious.

"What sort of gathering are we?" Dahlia asked the guide.

"Wait. You will see," he said.

After a time, and when dust sat in heaps on the shoulders and heads of most, one came to the front of the group. This one stood with the Great Fire behind and the boy thought he might catch fire.

"We are the Men," he said. Many of the gathered shouted it back or repeated it in whispers. The guide, sitting with Dahlia and the boy, shouted. The man raised one hand and the whispers and shouts ceased. "We are the Men, and today our purpose is renewed. The sea man has returned in the white shimmer to teach us the medicine for war-harm. Today, this island is saved."

The boy looked at Dahlia; his friend's eyes burned like the Great Fire. Sweat formed on Dahlia's head as this one spoke. The boy frowned at losing his friend.

The one speaking to shouts and whispers looked each of the gathered in the eye, one after the other. His eyes lowered and his hands folded at his heart.

"Bring out the ones who thought to leave," he said. "These look beyond the white shimmer for the medicine for war-harm. Do you gathered know the white shimmer is the sea man, and in the white shimmer is the fulfillment of the Men?"

Again, shouts and whispers.

"The wish of war-harm is for us gathered to be still, for the sneaking and hunting to cease, and for the white shimmer to disappear," the one said.

Shouts and whispers.

"Now you will see the executions," the guide said, baring his teeth in a smile to the boy and Dahlia.

Twenty-Five

"THE ONES WHO THOUGHT TO LEAVE . . . Now you will see the executions." The words rang in the boy's ears and the Great Fire burned loud and the boy sweat and looked about. He looked at the guide and thought his smile like that of three figures from the forest.

Executions? he thought. What could the Men mean in executions? Dahlia's eyes narrowed and his friend's brow furrowed, and he and Dahlia's eyes came together and went apart as fast. One at a time, grim Men were brought before the Great Fire. The one who spoke to shouts and whispers looked at each and kept his hands folded at his heart.

"These," the guide said to the two, "have thought to leave. After we dunk our heads and dance and have a meal, they will die. Before the sneaking and hunting, our home must be cleansed of any who would do us harm and spread lies. These are such. The white shimmer serves."

"They will die?" Dahlia asked.

"They will die," the guide said. "They would leave here and spread lies and slander the white shimmer. You saw the white shimmer. These would have our forest homes torn and the Great Fire unattended and they would let the island forget the white shimmer. We would never know the medicine for war-harm."

Dahlia's eyes moved from the guide to the Men who would die and back to the guide and to the Great Fire, which burned loud. The boy thought his friend would leave here. He was sure

Dahlia would distrust the Men and see the white shimmer charmed them.

The guide rose and approached the one who spoke to shouts and whispers and the two Men spoke and looked at the boy and Dahlia. The boy sweat and his hands shook and he saw Dahlia still sweat and now shook and the Great Fire burned loud.

The boy thought the gathering a bad dream, like the one with the turtles and the lake of fire. Would the Men execute ones who would leave? He had not seen death and thought not to see it today and looked for a way to remove himself from this place. None might notice, he and Dahlia being at the back of the gathering. The guide and the one who spoke to shouts and whispers still looked, though. If they would turn away, the boy thought, I could sneak back toward the forest homes and disappear into the green blackness.

The sun sank and hotter and hotter the air became. The two Men did not look away; the boy and Dahlia sweat more and shook more, and the Great Fire burned loud. All waited with slow dust gathering on their heads and shoulders. Those who would leave stood near the Great Fire with sad eyes and empty skin. The boy thought they looked already executed.

When the guide returned, he said, "We will serve you first."

Strange perfumes swirled with the dust and the boy was glad to have a meal before leaving.

"First," he said, "you will dunk your heads. Come."

He took the boy and Dahlia by the hands and the three walked through the gathered to a tall water bath. Even with the executions, both the boy and Dahlia smiled thinking about cooling from the Great Fire.

They stood before the tall water bath and the guide said, "Watch. I will go first."

Strange perfumes swirled with the dust and the boy's nose and throat burned with a new perfume.

The guide went and the boy thought the dunked had wild eyes.

"Who will go?" the dunked asked.

Dahlia stepped forward. Seconds felt as hours, and the boy watched Dahlia dunk and return with wild eyes and burning coughs and shouts from the gathered. The boy thought Dahlia was crying, and he stepped to take Dahlia's hand but found the hot edge of the bath. The gathered cheered and the boy thought the tall water bath not water and he dunked his head. There was no cooling or relief from the heat in this bath, only the burning of the Great Fire in his eyes and ears and nose and throat. The boy coughed with his head dunked and his throat filled and he swallowed, and he felt his own eyes turn wild and he thought the tall bath not water.

The boy returned and the gathered shouted and still seconds felt as hours, and now he could not see one thing and his mind wandered. He tried to see Dahlia, but his wild eyes could not see one thing. The Great Fire burned loud in his eyes and mouth and throat and stomach. He wondered if he might run to the not-so-distant lake and dunk there, though he felt like the burning might now follow him.

The boy surveyed the clearing of the Great Fire and thought it swayed like the sea. The gathered dipped and turned like one piece of sea moss cast to the current.

Words spoken to the boy and Dahlia, the guide took them to their place within the gathered. The boy thought the Men marveled at them, but he could not see one thing. He could not speak with the burning in his throat and stomach, and Dahlia's eyes looked as wild as his felt, and he wondered what Dahlia was thinking and how he might leave if he could not see one thing.

Sitting now, the boy felt like he saw the clearing before. He swayed like the sea and dipped and turned like a piece of sea moss cast to the current, and he put his fingertips to the floor and righted himself. He looked at Dahlia and smiled to comfort his friend's wild eyes.

Shouts and whispers.

A grey forest deer was brought before the gathered and the boy closed his eyes and opened them and did this many times to see if the grey forest deer stood before them, and it must have because it was there each time he opened. He looked at Dahlia, and his friend's eyes opened and closed too. Their eyes came together.

He looked at the sweating guide with wild eyes and thought his smile like the three figures from the forest.

The one who spoke to shouts and whispers again spoke, but the boy could not hear him. He felt far away and, only now able to see one thing, he looked at the grey forest deer. The boy closed his eyes and thought he was drifting on the sea above a reef and saw a grey forest deer there with him. He put his hands on the side of the forest deer. The boy understood, beyond sight and smell and sound and taste, the forest deer. He felt the heart jump and lungs fill and empty. He felt the muscle and skin and fur and understood the forest deer as he understood himself. It wasn't grey fur to marvel or a perfume to smell or a friend to drift with; this grey forest deer was alive! It breathed and moved and created beauty on the sea, above the reef. Without this creature, grey and large and quiet with white and brown spots, the sea would not exist as it is. The sun would not smell so and the salt water would not taste so and the sunrise fish would not be so. The sun and salt water and sunrise fish and sea moss and coral and sand and all the sea with all its reefs would not exist in song as they do without this grey forest deer.

The boy opened his eyes and felt woken from a dream. Two Men led the ancient and special in a circle around the Great Fire and brought it before the one who spoke to shouts and whispers. This one held a long spear. The boy's hands shook and sweat ran his face.

He looked at Dahlia and Dahlia at him, and Dahlia smiled, perhaps to comfort his wild eyes and shaking hands.

The one who spoke to shouts and whispers spoke again, but the boy was still far away. The spear plunged into the side of the grey forest deer and the boy closed his eyes and was again drifting on the sea above a reef with his hands on its side. It looked at him and he saw himself in the eyes of the creature, there on the sea.

The boy opened his eyes and the Great Fire burned loud and the grey and large and quiet tried to run, but the spear was all the way through. The grey fur and brown and white spots were now painted the deepest red—deeper than Punica—the boy had seen. The forest deer blinked so fast and let out such a wail the boy's sweat turned to silent tears and his hands and heart shook.

He looked at the guide; his smile was like that of the figures from the forest. Dahlia's silent eyes, welling with pained tears, remained on the spear sticking from the side of the forest deer, now painted in blood.

Still, the clearing swayed like the sea and the gathered dipped and turned like a piece of sea moss cast to the current.

With silent tears and shaking hands and heart, the boy watched the grey forest deer lose life and fall on the spear, and the gathered shouted and whispered, though the boy heard none. It was lifted above the Great Fire and a foul odor filled the clearing, and one after the other, all the Men dunked their heads.

The Men danced as the forest deer burned and the boy and Dahlia sat on the side. The guide understood and told the two to rest if they felt unwell. The boy wondered why the others could dance after dunking and he and Dahlia felt unwell.

His eyes still wild and his nose and mouth and throat still burning, the boy said, "Dahlia, we must leave here."

"I saw the white shimmer," Dahlia said. "I felt its beauty."

"This is not beauty," the boy said. "I touched the grey forest deer that day. I felt its heart and lungs and skin and muscle and fur. Why did the Men kill it?"

"I feel unwell," Dahlia said.

"And what of the executions?" the boy asked.

"I feel unwell."

The guide approached the boy and Dahlia. "If you feel unwell and resting does not help, dunk your heads again. It will relieve."

"It will relieve?" Dahlia asked, wiping dust and tears away.

"All feel unwell with one dunk."

"I will wait," the boy said.

The guide took Dahlia's hand and the boy watched his friend dunk again. The guide took Dahlia and joined the dance and the boy sat alone, feeling unwell with wild eyes. He saw the grey forest deer and smelled the strange perfumes swirling with the dust and heard the dancing of the Men and Dahlia and he wished the two had not come here.

Dahlia went for a third dunk and the boy thought more dunks must help, but the clearing swayed like the sea, and he thought only to sit. He called to his friend in the dance, but none heard him; the Great Fire burned loud. The boy saw Dahlia go for another dunk and another, and he thought now would be a good time to leave, but still the clearing swayed and he thought not to leave Dahlia with the Men and the Great Fire.

The dance stopped long after sunset and the grey forest deer was carved like fresh fruit and passed between each of the Men. Dahlia and the guide encouraged the boy to taste it.

"I feel unwell."

"You should dunk again and taste the meat," the guide said.

"You should dunk again and taste the meat," Dahlia said.

"I will rest now and dunk again soon. After I will taste the grey forest deer," the boy said, lying in the dust and dirt.

Dahlia smiled at him with wild eyes and the boy thought to cry for his friend eating the grey forest deer, but tears did not come. Still his eyes and nose and throat and stomach burned from one dunk.

"It tastes as beautiful as the white shimmer's song looked," Dahlia said.

"The sea man is in the white shimmer, our purpose fulfilled," the guide said. "This forest and all things of it serve to fulfill our purpose. This meat serves us."

"My friend will dunk again and taste the meat," Dahlia said, smiling.

The boy saw the wild eyes of the guide and Dahlia and felt his own and saw the lifeless eyes of the grey forest deer lying at the foot of the Great Fire. He knew the Men meant to execute those who thought to leave and wondered if he would be executed if he were caught leaving.

The boy's stomach burned as loud as the Great Fire and he thought to dunk again. Dahlia and the guide were smiling and talking as friends. The perfume swirled with the dust and he saw the lifeless eyes of the grey forest deer and saw the gathered tasting the meat and he knew he must not dunk again.

"When the gathered finish tasting the meat, the executions," the guide said, forest deer hanging from his teeth.

Dahlia smiled with the dancing and now the meat, and the boy thought his friend not bothered by the executions.

"They have spread lies and wish the white shimmer gone?" Dahlia asked.

"Yes," the guide said. "These would have no medicine for war-harm. What is our island without the white shimmer?"

Beautiful, the boy thought.

The gathered finished tasting the meat and the one who spoke to shouts and whispers again stood before the Great Fire. He spoke to those soon to be executed, each after the other. The boy's throat and stomach burned but the clearing did not sway like before, and he sat to see what would happen.

The boy looked at each of those to be executed and felt sad. "How will they die?" he asked.

None heard him and his imagination wandered the black and green and fiery place. The bloodied spear lay near the Great Fire.

He examined the sad eyes and empty skin and saw one familiar.

"My brother," he said.

Twenty-Six

HIS FATHER AND MOTHER swayed under the emerald light and he sat on their sitting place, watching the small claws practice their own sneaking and hunting. His brother appeared from the water, clutching a sea star.

"Mother, a sea star!" his brother said.

The boy leapt from their sitting place. "How far did you go, brother?" he asked.

"I went past the tall sea grass until the floor was gone," his brother said.

"Past the tall sea grass?"

"I have never been so far. I dove until I found the bottom, and the sea star and sand floor were all I saw."

"Let's go there," the boy said.

"You are small and the sea is dark now. I will show you past the tall sea grass one day," his brother said.

The boy held the sea star and laughed at it and asked to keep it but his father said it belonged in the sea. He went back to their sitting place and lay on the floor and wondered about the sea and the forest and the world beyond these. My brother knows adventure, the boy thought. One day I will join him in the sea and we will find smooth shells for mother and more sea stars and we will see what else is past the tall sea grass.

His brother came and sat with the boy, and the two watched their father and mother sway in the emerald light. They wondered aloud if their father had gone into the sea or the forest and what he found. These two longed for adventure.

His brother told the boy stories of the Men and the sneaking and hunting and said they lived in the forest. The boy did not know any lived in the forest until his brother said so.

"They sleep in the palms and live with no fathers or mothers," his brother would say.

"Who gathers fresh fruits and ripe nuts, and who do the Men sit with to learn?" the boy would ask.

"The forest gives the Men more fresh fruits and ripe nuts than you and I have ever seen," his brother would say. "And they are wise. They do not need to sit with any to learn."

"I would like to meet the Men," the boy would say.

"Someday you and I will join them."

Twenty-Seven

"MY BROTHER," the boy said again.

"Where?" Dahlia asked.

"He is to die."

The guide frowned. "It may not be your brother," he said.

"It is. May I speak to him?"

"We renounce our old," the guide said. "It may be your brother, or it may not be. He would not say if he saw you and would deny if you saw him."

The boy stood and walked through the Men gathered toward those to die. None stopped him. The guide and Dahlia stayed and the man who spoke to shouts and whispers watched with wild eyes. He rested his chin on his hand and allowed the boy to approach.

Each of the sad eyes followed the boy to the end of their line and the Great Fire burned loud.

"My brother," the boy said.

"And mine," his brother said.

The two embraced and the Men whispered, but the one who spoke to shouts and whispers raised a hand. They stopped.

"You thought to leave the Men?"

"Have you dunked your head in the ferment?" his brother asked.

A familiar safety came over the boy and tears cleared the wild from his eyes. He no longer felt the forest or the Men or the Great Fire or the ferment or the lifeless eyes of the grey forest deer. He was on their sitting place, watching his father and mother sway under the emerald light, and he was standing on the sand laughing at the sea star. The Joy of Senses came over him and he tasted the air in the emerald night of the sea and heard his own laugh and saw the pretty sway of his father and mother and the boy's brother took his hands. He was back in the clearing of the Great Fire with the Men and Dahlia and his brother, but he was lost in the song of that emerald night when his brother appeared with the sea star.

"Father is wise," his brother said. "The sneaking and hunting are in vain. The white shimmer does not serve."

"I know the Joy of Senses," the boy said.

His brother smiled and laughed through tears, and the two were on their sitting place longing for adventure and wondering of the sea and the forest.

"I will die in the Joy of Senses," his brother said. "I will die and join the beauty of the island, and you will hear me sing in the music of the green and purple birds with bright orange feet and you will see me dance in the sunrise fish of the reefs, and I will be in the forest and on the gold sand and in the sea, and in the Joy of Senses you will find me alive."

"We can run," the boy said.

"From what should we run?"

The man who spoke to shouts and whispers came and took the boy by the arm and led him to the guide and Dahlia and he stood with closed eyes.

Two of the gathered rose and held one who would leave while the one who spoke to shouts and whispers came and held the spear to the Great Fire. The boy thought the spear would burn and all would live and he and those who would die would show the Men and Dahlia the Joy of Senses. The spear turned the color of the Great Fire and the gathered waited in silence.

Dust fell and the perfumes of all that had come and gone swirled with it.

One after the other had the spear of the Great Fire plunged into his heart.

The gathered sat in silence, and Dahlia smiled in the song of the ferment, a song of confusion and disassociation. The boy wondered if his friend knew the spear in the heart was killing those who would have left.

The one who held the spear of the Great Fire and who spoke to shouts and whispers stood before the boy's brother. As he did with each of the others, he lowered his head and spoke to the one to die and the one to die spoke back.

Head raised high and eyes lost of sadness, the boy's brother said, "In the Joy of Senses, you will find me alive."

The spear plunged into his heart. The boy stood with silent tears, and Dahlia winced and frowned and asked the guide what the boy's brother said.

"Lies. He slandered the white shimmer," the guide said.

The boy heard this and closed his wet eyes and saw his father and mother swaying under the emerald light. They stopped swaying, and his mother went to her knees and wept and his father looked to the sea for a son with a sea star who would not come.

The boy opened his wet eyes and went to his knees and wept, but none heard him.

"I will not stay here," he said. Again, none heard him.

"Friend, will you dunk your head with me?" Dahlia asked the boy.

"I will not," the boy said. "The Joy of Senses does not live here, Dahlia. War-harm lives here."

Dahlia stepped away and spun in the swirling dust, as one dancing might.

"Goodbye, Dahlia," the boy said with wet eyes. "My friend."

Twenty-Eight

THE BOY LEFT THE CLEARING of the Great Fire and wandered toward the not-so-distant lake and thought to dunk in the lake to clear his eyes and nose and throat and stomach of the ferment and the dust and tears. The emerald light was above the forest canopy, and the boy wondered how his brother and the others had been caught leaving. He wondered if they spoke the truth of the white shimmer to others loyal to the Men. He thought it easy to leave and wished his brother had left at night when the Men were lost in the song of the ferment.

Coming to the lake, the boy sat where he had with the guide and Dahlia. He saw a sleeping turtle and thought to bring the turtle with him and realized he did not know where he would go. He could go home to the gold sand or to the orchard of palms as tall as three and smooth, fine sand or beyond this to the blue rock mountains.

He wondered of Albahr and the white bird which spoke man and thought he would like to see them again. More than the gold sand or the orchard of palms as tall as three or the blue rock mountains or Albahr and the white bird, the boy wanted to fall into the Joy of Senses again. He was not sure he ever would if the burning of the ferment stayed and if he never cleaned the dust from his hair.

The boy thought of the grey forest deer and was near tears when his dream friend, the white bird he longed to see, landed on the sleeping turtle.

"My friend," the boy said. "Dahlia is lost and my brother is gone and I do not know where to go and the ferment burns my eyes and nose and mouth and throat and stomach and my hair is covered in the dust of the Great Fire."

"Do not be afraid."

The boy wiped his face.

"None are lost and none are gone in the Joy of Senses," the white bird said. "You showed Dahlia the Joy of Senses. Your friend may find it again. Your brother did. And on him: he is not gone. Did you hear what he said to you?"

"He said in the Joy of Senses I would find him alive."

"Have you?" the white bird asked.

"There is only war-harm here," the boy said.

"Then we must leave. Go into the lake and come back new."

The moss along the not-so-distant lake was cool and wet and the boy thought it would make a nice place to sleep, but he wanted to clear his eyes and nose and throat and stomach of the ferment and the dust and the tears. He went in to his neck and dunked his head in the water and ran his hands through his hair and opened his eyes and mouth and let the water consume him until he was again only flesh and water. Had the white bird been another boy, he might have made sure the boy was alive. He stayed until his lungs shook. He stood and the water was at his neck, and he gasped and there was no more dust in his hair or tears in his eyes or ferment in his nose and mouth and throat and stomach.

"You are new," the white bird said when the boy came back.

"I am free of the dust and the ferment and my tears," the boy said. "I will rest, and at sunrise, we will go."

"We will go now, or your life will be left to the spear of the Great Fire," the white bird said.

"You will walk with me?"

"I will rest on your shoulder."

The boy and the white bird returned to the forest by the same felled-palm path he and Dahlia found the Men, and only when they came to a stream did the white bird permit the boy to rest.

The boy's mind wandered, and he could not sleep. "Let it wander aloud," the white bird said.

"I worry what will come of Dahlia."

"Rest."

His mind settled and his eyes fluttered and strange thoughts came and he knew he was soon to sleep. He saw the white shimmer, dancing about, chased by Dahlia. Then Dahlia chasing a grey forest deer. Then Albahr and his father and mother sitting on the gold sand of his home. Then the white bird carrying the Great Fire over the sea and dropping it, far away from the sand. Then Dahlia holding a sea star, smiling with affection at its pink and grey arms. He slept, smiling.

THE BOY WOKE in the warmth of the sun and found the forest lit by day. He was alone and felt the white bird would not return.

"Where will I go?"

He lay again in the sunned forest and closed his eyes with easy thoughts. The Great Fire was far away. He saw the taller and the freckled and Albahr and the white bird which spoke man, his dream friends, and the pretty basin and the cascade.

"I will return to the orchard of palms as tall as three." He stood and breathed fresh and deep.

Still, as he walked, the boy's mind wandered, and he could not fall into any song of the Joy of Senses. He thought of Dahlia and the white shimmer and his brother and father and mother and the grey forest deer and his dream friends and war-harm.

"War-harm threatens where any gather without the Joy of Senses. It is not an enemy from here or far, as the Men believe, but is within any carrying captivation other than in the Joy of Senses," the boy said. "The Men live in war-harm because they gather without the Joy of Senses; they are captive of the white shimmer. With the Great Fire, they know no quiet, and with their ferment they know no patience."

The boy felt sad and wished Dahlia walked with him and they could share a lime or a cobnut and he could talk of the Joy of Senses and his friend could talk of adventure.

"I must find the Joy of Senses again and fall into a song of the forest or orchard or cascade or a stream," the boy said. "Perhaps I will find Albahr at the basin with people of the palms as tall as three and he can help me."

With some time, the boy reached the basin. People were gathered, as when he and Dahlia first came. He sat among the fruit and nut trees and blossoms and, when Albahr came, at the back of the gathered. Albahr smiled at the boy before speaking.

"Friends," Albahr said. "Close your eyes. A breeze is here; let it whisper. Do you hear it?"

Albahr paused.

"Now let your lips come apart, friends. Let the breeze brush your lips and tap your tongue and feel it inside your mouth. Close your mouth and look inward. Watch the breeze escape through your nose and ears and feel it behind your eyes. Now, friends, breathe as soft as the breeze and taste the air. What is there?"

Again, Albahr paused.

"Punica and lemons. White sand and cool stream. I taste the cascade and rubyroot and the black dirt of the basin."

The boy did as Albahr spoke. He closed his eyes and let the breeze whisper and he heard it. The breeze whispered for the boy to wake. His senses came to life and his mind relaxed and he no longer thought of Dahlia and the white shimmer and his brother and father and mother and the grey forest deer and war-harm. His mind was still, and the breeze whispered.

The boy's lips came apart when Albahr spoke it. The breeze brushed his lips and tapped his tongue, and the boy felt the breeze inside his mouth. It was there, and his mind was still and he let the breeze whisper and brush and tap and fill without desire. The breeze came for all and the boy observed it with all.

The boy's mouth closed when Albahr spoke it and he looked inward. The turmoil and panic of the ferment and the white shimmer and the Great Fire was gone, though he did not notice. He thought not of these, only of the breeze. His body held the breeze and his mind was still. The breeze left through his nose and ears and he felt it behind his eyes as it left. His nose and ears came alive in cool sensation. His eyes felt flush with tears, though he was not sad. All was new again and his mind was still, and the breeze left him.

Again, the boy's lips came apart. His senses alive and his mind still, the boy found the air and tasted it. It filled with the perfumes of the basin and the orchard, pulled upward from the sand and downward from the sun. Perfumes shone as colors and shades of colors behind his closed eyes. His whole body felt to lift, and the boy smiled. His eyes and mouth and throat and stomach smiled for the air of the basin. He opened his ears back to the clearing and heard birds and winged insects and the buzzing of a yellow fly and, he thought, a forest moth's white wing flap. The cascade capered and dove and bubbled and splashed into the basin, lapping then at the black dirt.

The boy's hands went from his legs to the white sand floor of the clearing, and the fine sand went beneath his fingernails and it fell in drapes. When he shifted his buried hands, he thought the whole orchard rippled. The roots of each palm—stretching far from the basin in every direction—grew as one beneath where he sat. His hands found it, and he saw the whole orchard from the clearing. His eyes stayed and his smile grew.

The song of the basin rose within and outside the boy, and he was wrapped in the Joy of Senses again. He felt himself a palm as tall as three growing in this clearing, as if the entire life of the place and each of the others gathered was his own. He saw the river come from the blue rock mountains and cut through the orchard as a cascade and form the basin. He saw the water of the basin give life to the sand and turn it to black dirt, giving home to purple-veined rubyroot and blossoms and many other roots. Birds and winged insects carried seeds beyond the black dirt. The seeds took water from the basin and life from the sun and grew into Punica and lemon and cobnut and lime and chuara and blossoms and more. Birds and winged insects and the yellow fly and the forest moth came and took home about the trees and roots.

The boy smelled and tasted and saw and heard and felt. Each of these came back to the air. In the song of the basin, he forgot the ferment and the heat of the Great Fire and the sweat and shaking hands and his loss. He only knew love of others and the island and himself in the Joy of Senses.

The boy opened his eyes and was home in that still, hot air.

Twenty-Nine

THE BOY STAYED for many sunrises and sunsets with the people of the palms as tall as three. He loved them and loved the orchard and the whole island, though much of it was still unknown. He was fair to the palms as tall as three and the cascade and the winged insects and the birds he now knew well and, though none were green and purple with bright orange feet, he loved these.

The boy often sat with Albahr and watched a piece of their home and explored it from where they sat in the Joy of Senses. Or they would climb the blue rock mountains and explore those (and those held much to explore), but they always explored by sitting and observing in the Joy of Senses. The two, and the white bird always resting on Albahr's or now the boy's shoulder, did not move even a cone from the tall pines of the blue rock mountains or disturb a rock set in its place.

"Leave this place as the Joy of Senses finds it," Albahr would say.

"Will we take this new nut or this new fruit?" the boy might ask. He often thought of the curiosity of the taller or the freckled when he and Albahr and the white bird explored something new.

"Taste them here, observe them, and fall into the song of these mountains, but leave them. Allow them to rest in the song they help create."

The boy's love for the island and the people of the palms as tall as three grew and often he sat, at times for three sunrises and sunsets, in the Joy of Senses. Palms became friends singing, and moss and rocks and fruits and nuts instruments in the melody of a song the boy experienced each sunrise, through his days, and at sunset.

He did not return to the forest, though he longed for its song, for many sunrises and sunsets. The place felt distant and plagued. Still, the boy yearned for the forest he and Dahlia knew and walked.

He often thought of Dahlia and wondered if any would return from the Men and bring word of his friend, but none came.

He studied the Joy of Senses and lived in constant song and always observed, never interrupting person or palm or rock or cascade or breeze. Listening and looking and smelling and tasting and feeling grew the beauty of the island and of the people of the palms as tall as three.

"Albahr," the boy said one day. "I grow as wise as my father."

"What is wisdom, friend?" Albahr asked.

"Wisdom is seeing in the Joy of Senses, hearing in the Joy of Senses, tasting in the Joy of Senses, smelling in the Joy of Senses, and feeling with the love of the Joy of Senses; it is the heart beating with love of oneself, others, and the island. My wise father had it, and now I feel it inside me," the boy said.

"Where did you learn this?" Albahr asked.

"I have learned it all my life and did not understand any of it until I was captivated in the Joy of Senses. I am captive to observation and experience and sensation; in these, I have become wise. I suppose I did not learn it at all, then."

"You, friend, are wise," Albahr said. "And what does wisdom tell you?"

"It tells me what I have already seen, though it tells me with light shone into shadows. War-harm, I understand, is only a lack of love of oneself and others and the island. The Joy of Senses is the medicine for war-harm, and in the Joy of Senses, one will never die. One falls into the island and joins the song of his home. The people of the palms as tall as three will fall into the island and become a new palm as tall as three or another caper of the cascade or a winged insect's buzz in which another will find love. Grey forest deer fall into the island and join the song of the forest in a rubyroot patch or the loo of a night bird or a stream which wets moss for a wanderer to sleep on and fall into the song of the night forest."

"You are wise," Albahr said.

"My brother died by the spear of the Great Fire," the boy said. "In his death among the Men, he told me this, but I did not understand. Now I do. He fell and has returned to the gold sand of our home. I will hear him in the music of the green and purple birds with bright orange feet and I will smell him in the soft breeze filling our sturdy wood home and I will taste him in the kiwis and I will feel him as I lie in the warmth of the sun. Without the Joy of Senses, there is death. With the Joy of Senses, there is the song of all that has passed and lives now and will come to pass. It is beautiful. It binds all to one another and all to the island and the island to all. Captivation elsewhere is death and war-harm."

"You are wise. Go to the green and purple birds with bright orange feet."

Thirty

THE BOY WAS PATIENT in walking through the forest. He stopped often and rested long, always falling into a song with the Joy of Senses. He longed to see the grey forest deer again and to hear the night bird's loos and to taste fresh rubyroot from beside a cool stream, so he walked with ease and light steps and never moved through an area without an appreciation for its song.

The boy thought to go see the Men, and he wondered if the three figures would come for him in the night, but he thought the Men might execute him and he did not see the three figures. He looked at his hands and gone were the hands of a boy, and he wondered if, because his hands could not be recognized, would the Men or the three figures know his face. But the boy met neither as he walked through the forest.

When the forest air carried salt and the black dirt of the floor was spotted with sand, the boy knew his home was near. His heart beat fast and after a short time, he saw the forest edge and their sturdy wood home.

The boy went right into their wood home and found gold sand piled in the corners and their sitting place crooked. His mother's baskets were stacked and when the boy lifted these, small claws scurried.

"My father and mother are gone, and my brother is gone," the boy said. A tear walked his cheek, but he smiled.

The boy walked to the sea and sat in a sea pool. Three green and purple birds with bright orange feet came and tapped the cool sand near him. One splashed in his pool and the boy smiled for their music. It rested on the boy's ears, and he closed his eyes and the salt air filled his nose. It came and rested in his mouth and on his throat, and he was filled with the perfumes of their home: kiwis and sun chuara and other fresh fruits and ripe nuts. His hands touched the sand and he saw himself seated with his father and watching his mother. He heard their laughs and his brother's laugh in the music of the green and purple birds with bright orange feet. Their laughs were so clear and bright he thought if he opened his eyes, the three would be standing before him and they would all rest and enjoy a kiwi and talk of the adventures had. His smile grew, and he felt the warmth of the sun and expressed thanks for the warmth, and the boy knew his father and mother and brother were not gone.

"It is no felled palm, rot and dead, but this soft breeze smells wonderful."

The boy turned his head and saw, spinning in the warmth of the sun with arms stretched, a girl with dark hair and eyes like the night bird's loos. One arm held the stems of rubyroot.

"Will rubyroot grow in this gold sand?" the girl asked. She stopped spinning and smiled at the boy.

"Dahlia."

"My friend."

THE END

Want more *Green and Purple Birds with Bright Orange Feet*?

Visit BIRDS.GEORGECALLAHANAUTHOR.COM for a
FREE short story, *Albahr's Sermon*.

You can make a big difference.

Reviews help other readers find my books. If you have two minutes, please let me know what you thought of *Green and Purple Birds with Bright Orange Feet* by visiting

REVIEW.GEORGECALLAHANAUTHOR.COM

You can help other readers find their Joy of Senses.

Thank you for your two minutes,

George

About the Author

George Callahan was born in Cleveland, Ohio. He is an ultramarathon runner and fiction writer. His books often draw on principles of ultramarathon running. adventure, purpose, community, and challenge. Other inspirations include lyrical music, whimsical television shows, and writers such as Ernest Hemingway.

Green and Purple Birds with Bright Orange Feet, George's first novel, deals primarily with the issues of addiction and possession in a world full of natural sensation. Like many of George's books, it is an appeal for thoughtfulness and curiosity.

Readers of adventure novels, romance, quests, and allegorical fiction will enjoy the characters and stories George creates in writing.

George lives in Raleigh, North Carolina, with his dog, Cowboy.

Connect with George at GeorgeCallahanAuthor.com or on Instagram @fictionGeorge

Take a picture with your book and use #JoyOfSenses on Instagram.

Made in the USA
Monee, IL
18 December 2023

49492187R00090